THE WOLF FORSAKEN

RITE WORLD 7: RITE OF THE WOLF

JULIANA HAYGERT

COPYRIGHT

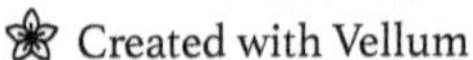 Created with Vellum

AUTHOR'S NOTE

I hope you enjoy reading *The Wolf Forsaken*!

Don't forget to sign up for my Newsletter to find out about new releases, cover reveals, giveaways, and more!

If you want to see exclusive teasers, help me decide on covers, read excerpts, talk about books, etc, join my reader group on Facebook: Juliana's Club!

RITE WORLD

Welcome to the RITE WORLD!

Free Novella:
The Vampire Hunt

Rite World:
The Vampire Heir (Book 1)
The Witch Queen (Book 2)
The Immortal Vow (Book 3)
The Warlock Lord (Book 4)
The Wolf Consort (Book 5)
The Crystal Rose (Book 6)
The Wolf Forsaken (Book 7)
The Fae Bound (Book 8)
The Blood Pact (Book 9)

Rite World: Blackthorn Hunters Academy

The Demons Kiss (Book 1)
The Hunter Secret (Book 2)
The Soul Bond (Book 3)
The Shadow Trials (Book 4)
The Immortal Vow (Book 5)

And more to come!

THE VAMPIRE HUNT

I have an exclusive novella set in the Rite World that is just for my newsletter subscribers!

Click here to sign-up and receive your book!

THE VAMPIRE HUNT
A Rite World Novella

Norah is a demon hunter, one of the best graduated from the Blackthorn Hunters Academy. When she's sent to investigate a case concerning demons in a small town, she runs into a very arrogant vampire. Her first instinct is to kill him, after all, he's a supernatural and demon hunters are taught to end all evil.

Cain is a vampire prince. Because of his status, he's in charge of making sure humans don't find out about his kind. During a routine investigation, he bumps into a very sexy demon hunter and he wonders what she's doing on his way.

However, the case grows much bigger for Norah and Cain to handle alone. To find the truth and win this battle, the vampire and the demon hunter will have to hunt together —without killing each other.

How well could this end?

1

THE LANDSCAPE OUTSIDE LOOKED JUST LIKE MY HEART.

Cold, harsh, and buried underneath a ton of snow.

I clutched my mug full of steaming hawthorn tea with both hands and brought it to my lips, my eyes fixed on the view—a small valley and beyond it a mountain chain, with the sun dipping below it, staining the sky with rose and orange tints.

I knew I should have stuck to warmer places, where no one would guess a frost fae was hiding. I tried to. First, I hid in Florida, then Alabama, then Texas. I even tried hiding in Mexico. The heat in those places was too much for me to bear. Even northern California could be too warm for me.

So, over two years ago, I ended up moving north, to Montana, where the seasons were more pronounced, though it never got as hot as the south. But it got cold, too cold for the shadow fae. I was confident that here, deep into a frozen forest, hidden in a small cottage in the middle of nowhere, Prince Lark wouldn't be able to find me.

I let out a long sigh, tired of being alone, of feeling lonely, but without a choice. If I left this cottage, if I tried to live in a normal town, I would be found.

A knock came from the door.

My heart stopped and the mug slipped from my hand, crashing on the crude wooden floor, and spilling hot liquid everywhere.

Channeling my magic, I positioned myself in the middle of the small one-room cottage. Whoever was here, hadn't come because they were lost in the woods. They were here because they had come for me.

But how the hell had they found me?

"Open the door, Farrah, before I break it down."

My magic slipped from my veins.

In four large steps, I reached the door and opened it. Eyes wide, I stared at my brother. "Daleigh."

I hadn't seen him in so long, but he hadn't changed much. His fair skin seemed paler than before, and his white hair was longer, almost at his waist, but his blue eyes remained the same—cold and serious. Though his clothes had changed completely. Before, he used to wear his full armor, but now he wore gray pants, a thick white sweater, and a long white coat. At least the colors continued the same.

"I should give you props for hiding so well," he said, walking past me, and examining the cottage.

I suddenly felt conscious of the tiny placed around us,

and the mess I rarely tidied up. Deciding I didn't care about his opinion, I puffed out my chest and asked, "How did you find me?"

Daleigh stopped, ran a finger over the dusty countertop of the corner kitchen, and raised his eyes at me. "I've been trying to find you since you ran away."

I averted my gaze, remembering when and why I left everyone behind.

If only I hadn't taken that dagger, if only I hadn't made that damned deal. I exhaled, telling myself for the hundredth time that I shouldn't cry for things I couldn't change.

I just had to keep on walking.

"So what? You've come to take me?"

Daleigh's hand clenched for a moment, before he opened and wiggled his fingers, trying to contain whatever feeling he didn't want to show me. "Farrah, I don't think I need you to remind you of your own deal. The three years are almost up. You have to go back now."

"I don't *have* to do anything," I said.

I took a step back, putting more distance between ourselves. Daleigh was older than me and a true warrior. I might be a powerful fae, but he was stronger than me. If he decided to take me by force, I wouldn't be able to win against him.

"Farrah, please, you know what is at stake here," Daleigh said, his voice low, pleading. "If you marry Prince Lark, he'll forgive us. His father will let us go back to the fae realm. That's what we all want, right? That's what we've always wanted." His shoulders lowered one inch. "Can't you do that for our people?"

My stomach knotted.

He couldn't put this on me, damn it.

Long ago, our people were banished to the human world with no way of going back. If I went through with the plan, if I stopped running, our people would be able to return.

"You know it isn't that simple," I whispered, wishing my brother would stand with me just this once. "You're asking me to sacrifice myself."

But he only hardened. "For our people. Believe me, if I could have made a deal like that, I would have. I would gladly marry a whale if that meant my people and I could return to our home."

"I'm not you, Daleigh," I barked, my voice rising with my temper. "Besides, I was pushed away from our people, remember? I was handed to witches and left to die. I don't care about our people!"

Daleigh flinched. Of course he remembered. He had been the one to send me away. And now here he was, begging me to help him. Pathetic.

"That was a mistake," he said, his voice low. "I wish I could go back in time and found a better way to deal with all that was happening."

And I wanted to go back in time and undo the deal I had struck. I deeply regretted what I had done for Luana, the werewolf who was now the alpha of the Starlight pack.

Almost three years ago, I helped her steal the Dagger of All Hunting from Prince Lark's fortress. However, the stealing part didn't go too well. We ended up caught. Prince Lark, prince of the Shadow fae, whose father ruled the fae realm, had always been very fond of me, so I used that to our advantage. I promised him I would marry him in three years time.

Of course, I never had any intention of marrying him.

That was why I ran away.

That was why I left Wyatt behind.

Sometimes, I wondered how he was doing. Was he living with Luana and Keeran, helping them with the Starlight pack and the warlocks? Had he found a pretty werewolf and settled down?

My heart squeezed with the thought. Though I wanted him to be happy, it hurt me to think he had found someone.

Someone other than me.

I shook my head, sending all those troubling images away. "It's too late. I'm not going anywhere."

Daleigh stalked to me, towering me by an entire head. "My dear sister, I love you very much, but I won't stand for this. You have a few days to change your mind. I hope you make the right choice."

He started walking past me.

I asked, "Or what?"

Daleigh glanced at me over his shoulder. "Or I'll take you to Prince Lark by force."

I gasped. Deep down, I thought, hoped, he would never

do that. But looking now at his icy blue eyes, I knew he would.

Without another word, or threat, Daleigh walked out of the cottage, slamming the door behind him.

I put a hand over my racing heart and tried breathing in and out, calming myself down. But my feelings became a turmoil and I had to sit down on the low couch to catch my breath, to process my thoughts.

My own brother would take me to an evil fae prince to save the people that once shunned me away? Was he for real?

I didn't care about any of that.

I wouldn't allow myself to be dragged away like that. To be handed to Prince Lark like a grand price.

I waited for about one hour, to make sure Daleigh had really left, then I jumped into action. As fast as I could, I packed some food, water, and clothes, put on a heavy coat over my shoulder, and left the cottage.

Once more, I was on the run.

2

WYATT

I FOLLOWED THE DEMON INTO THE DARKNESS.

The demon, shapeshifted as a male human in his early thirties, hadn't realized I knew its secret. It thought it was tricking me, as it did with all of its victims. Usually, I didn't get involved with messes like this, but when I saw the demon going for an innocent girl just outside a pub, a girl with hair so blond it was almost white, something snapped in me. I couldn't let this fucking demon kill her.

So I pretended to be a regular human, drunk and ready for a brawl, and pushed the girl away. I noticed the disappointment in the demon's dark eyes when it got me instead of the girl, but it was short lived. At least, it had a victim.

Or so it thought.

The moment I stepped into the dark alley behind it, snow crunching under my feet, I began stripping off my clothes. When the demon turned around, I was stark naked—what? I didn't want to ruin yet another pair of pants.

"I know what you are," I said, before shifting.

My limbs stretched, my muscles grew harder, and fur covered my skin. In wolf form, I bared my fangs at the demon.

It too shapeshifted. The human skin peeled away like a carcass, revealing a long body with thin limbs, translucent skin that hugged big bones, and a face that reminded me of a skull.

Suddenly, I had only one instinct: to kill. Adrenaline filled my veins. With no patience for playing its game, I lunged at the demon, going directly for its throat. A second later, the demon was on the cold ground, his throat ripped open, blood seeping in a wide pool around it.

Slowly, I backed away from its body, but I didn't avert my eyes.

This was the only high of my life, the only thing I did well in the past two, three years.

It should disgust me. It did in the beginning. But now I was so far gone, I couldn't remember how I was before.

Unless I remembered *her*.

So I didn't. Every time thoughts of the past, memories of her, snaked into my mind, I pushed them away. I shut my fucking brain down, not willing to go that rabbit hole again.

I was about to shift back into my human form when a yelp reached my wolf ears. A woman was pushed into the dark alley by two strong men. One had a hand over her mouth, while the other held her waist, guiding her to him. She jerked, trying to get rid of them, but the men only laughed and groped her more.

They pushed her against the wall.

My naturally hot temper spiked and I saw only red in front of me. With the adrenaline of the previous murder still running high in my veins, I turned to the new threat.

Stepping out of the shadows, I snarled at the men.

They froze, staring at me with wide eyes.

"Is that ... is that a wolf?" one of the men asked, his voice trembling.

"A wolf in town? That's crazy," the other one said. Though his voice was steady, I could smell the fear in him from a mile away.

I snarled again, showing even more of my fangs.

The men, now concerned with me, forgot about the woman. After slipping on the snow, she ran from the alley.

Good, now I could do what I wanted.

"Nice wolfie," one of the men said, his hand out as if to ward me off.

What a motherfucker.

Without warning, I leaped on them.

And I killed them.

THE WIND BLEW EVEN COLDER OUTSIDE OF TOWN. AS I walked into the woods, I zipped up my jacket until the collar covered my mouth, but that wasn't enough against this fucking cold. I fished the wool beanie from my pocket and put it over my messy hair, then shoved my hands into gloves.

I could have stayed in town, rented a loft, like I used to do, but that had been a lifetime ago, it seemed. I had changed a lot since three years ago, and I had changed a lot more in the last two.

Sometimes, I looked at my hands, usually covered in someone else's blood, and I didn't recognize myself.

What the fuck was I doing?

I had lost myself along the way and now I didn't know what was left or right anymore. All I cared about was killing scumbags who didn't deserve to take a next breath, and hiding in the woods, where I could be a werewolf without shame.

A lone wolf.

Despite myself, unwelcomed thoughts filled my mind. My pack, Dark Vale, had been destroyed a handful of years ago, and Luana became the alpha of the Starlight pack, a group of magical werewolves. She had invited me to stay with her and Keeran, a warlock and her mate, but how could I when I was so different from anyone else there?

But sometimes I wondered, what would have happened to me if I had stayed? Would I have a place? Would I be with Farrah? Would I have become the fucking murderer I was now?

I didn't know, and I didn't care.

Because if I cared, I would go crazy.

I marched deeper into the woods and made my way

into the small cave I called home. Here, I knew the risk of bumping into someone was minimal, since no one would brave the snow and cold, at least during the winter months.

I took off my coat and my gloves and sat before the unlit fire in the center of the dark cave. I quickly lighted it and placed the leftover hare I had caught the other day over it. It was already cooked, but warm meat would be better than cold.

Like an animal, I devoured the rest of the hare. The cave echoed as I got up and washed my hands with the water from a bottle. There was a stream nearby, but it was frozen at this time of the year, so I bought bottled water and kept it under several hides to keep it warm so it wouldn't freeze too.

Silence fell once again when I lay down on one of the hides—my bed. I stared at the ceiling, the shadows from the small fire dancing against the rock. It was the middle of the day, but I didn't care. I didn't have anything better to do and I was fucking tired.

I closed my eyes.

And all I saw was blood.

Ripped throats, open guts, terrified faces. The screams filled my head.

Breathing hard, I sat up.

Nightmares assaulted me every fucking night, why wasn't I used to them by now?

I looked around the cave. The fire had died out and only a few embers braved the cold. Groaning, I stood and went to the fire. I better start it again before I froze in my sleep.

My ears prickled and I halted mid-step.

Voices filtered in the distance, too far for human ears, but not for werewolves.

Then a scream.

I shook my head. Whatever was happening, whoever was in danger, was at least two miles out. It didn't affect me.

A new scream chilled my bones.

What the fuck? Knowing I wouldn't be able to go back to sleep, I grabbed my thick coat and marched into the snow.

3

FARRAH

WHOSE IDEA HAD IT BEEN TO AVOID MAIN ROADS AND WALK through the forest? The snow didn't bother me, nor did the cold, but the distance, the damn time it took to cross the woods on foot was ridiculous.

I had been walking for over a day, making sure to cover my tracks so Daleigh, or anyone else couldn't find me. But this was too much. I veered toward one of the less used highways, intend on hitchhiking, or even stealing—borrowing—a car so I could get to the nearest international airport faster.

My plan was to go to Europe. I doubted having an entire ocean among us would stop Prince Lark, or even Daleigh, from coming after me, but it should make it harder. I hoped.

The highway was more deserted than I expected. I reached it, halted beside it, and waited for a car to drive by. None came. Tired and starving, I continued walking along the road, hoping a car would show up soon, and be nice enough to take me in.

In five hours, three cars drove by, and the three of them ignored me completely.

I dragged my feet for another two hours, before giving up for the day. The sun was starting to go down, shining over the snow and lending it a goldish glow. I didn't want to stop by the edge of the forest and sleep under a cold, wet tree. This time, I would rent a room at a roadside motel, even if only for a few hours, so I could eat, take a shower, and rest a little, before continuing my march toward freedom.

The sun continued moving slow, but the world around me darkened faster. Unnaturally.

Oh shit. I knew what that meant. Despite my exhaustion and my aching legs, I ran. Then I heard them, coming right behind me, making the world dark in their wake. I forgot about the road and jumped back among the trees.

I just hoped that with the snow all around me, I could boost my magic. I knew I couldn't kill them, they were too powerful for me, but I could try to get away.

As fast as I could with my feet sinking into the fluffy snow, I weaved among the trees, going deeper into the forest.

Then they appeared in front of me.

I skidded to a stop, almost face-planting on the snow. My blood rushed in my ears, my heart beating fast. It was a trap. The ones chasing me purposefully brought me here, where I was now surrounded by them.

Six shadow fae.

Though I didn't recognize them, I was sure they had been sent by Prince Lark. Which meant, they couldn't hurt me. Well, they could, but they couldn't kill me. Prince Lark wanted me alive.

I called on my magic, feeling it alive inside me and all around me, in the snow, the icicles on the branches, and the chilly air.

"Stay back!" I shouted, raising my hands.

One of them peeled his lips back, showing me his teeth in a mix of a wicked smile and a snarl.

Enough! I pushed my hands forward, bringing ice shards the size of small daggers from the snow with me. I threw the shards at them.

Disappearing in the shadows, the fae dodged my strike. A moment later, they appeared again, closing in around me.

I gasped.

"Surrender if you don't want to get hurt," one of the fae said, his voice as oily as the shadows.

"Never," I said with a snarl.

I threw my hand out, sending a blast of snow over three of the fae. Not expecting the hit, they fell back, and I jumped over them, dashing away.

Running was futile, I knew that, but I couldn't just stay put and let them take me.

A shadow bolt grazed my arm and I screamed as it burned my skin just as much as fire. My steps faltered, both from the shallow wound and my exhaustion.

No, I had to keep going. I couldn't stop now. I just had to keep running, throwing what I had left of my powers at them, until they gave up.

Shit, they would never give up.

And yet, I ran.

A shadow fae popped in my path. My breath catching, I skid to a stop. I made it to turn and keep running, but the others were too fast. One of the shadow fae caught me from behind, closing his hand around my arm and tugging me back.

I jerked against his hold, though there was no strength left in me.

For good measure, the fae's hand sparked, teasing me with a shadow bolt. I screamed as the pain rocked my body and brought me down to my knees.

My vision blurred.

I was going to pass out. I was going to faint right here, and when I woke up, I would be in Prince Lark's Shade Fortress. I inhaled deeply, trying to restore my strength, but I could barely catch my breath.

"Let's go," the fae said, pulling me by the arm and dragging me through the snow.

A snarl echoed among the trees.

A second later, something jumped and attacked the shadow fae.

I fell on the snow as my kidnapper let go of me and turned to the new threat.

I blinked, trying to understand what was going on.

A blur of light brown fur flashed in my poor vision.

My heart skipped a beat.

Could it be?

"Wyatt?" I whispered, the adrenaline quickly leaving my body.

I sank into the darkness.

I WOKE UP WITH A START, CHANNELING MY MAGIC, READY TO defend myself from the shadow fae. My eyes bugged and my heart speeding up, I glanced around. I was in a cave, with several blankets over me.

What the hell?

"Hey, it's okay," a voice said. A voice rougher than I remembered, colder.

Slowly, I turned to the voice.

Wyatt sat a few feet from me, warming his hand in front of a small fire. I gaped at him, not believing my eyes. Wyatt had grown these past three years, bulked up. He had gone from a cute teenager to a full grown up with five o'clock shadow over his sharp jaw and chin, and long brown hair that grazed his wide shoulders.

He glanced at me, his hazel eyes shining with the orange light coming from the fire. "You're safe now."

I stared at him some more. "What are you doing here?"

A knot marred his forehead. "What are *you* doing here?"

I shook my head. It didn't make sense. I had seen Wyatt beside Luana and Keeran before I left. I had been sure he would be fine with them. That he had found his place and would serve a purpose. "I ... why aren't you at the Starlight Vale? Were you sent this way on a mission?"

Wyatt returned his gaze to the fire. "I left right after we defeated Isalia. I thought you had stayed."

"Ditto." I glanced around again, taking in the cave. Clothes piled at one corner, canned food and bottled water took another corner. "This is where you've been living all this time?"

Wyatt picked up a long stick and poked on the fire, stirring up some embers, and making the fire crackle. "No. At first, I tried living normally. But ..." He shrugged. "Things have changed." He turned his eyes to me. "What about you?"

"I've been hiding." I pushed the blankets off me, but quickly pulled them back when I saw my bare legs. "Where are my pants?"

"You fell on the snow," he told me. "Your jacket and your pants were wet. So were your boots. I took them off to get you warmer. They are dry now." He pointed to a pile of folded clothes to my left. I could see my coat, my pants, my socks, my boots, and my bag. Wyatt cleared his throat. "And don't worry, I didn't see anything." Still, my cheeks flamed with the idea of Wyatt peeling my pants. Wyatt jerked his chin at me. "You were saying ... ?"

"Right, hm." I frowned, chasing my train of thought. "I thought that if I stayed in Starlight Vale, Prince Lark would find me too easily. So I left. And I've been hiding ever since."

"So, those fae who attacked last night? They were the prince's men?"

I nodded. "The time is coming up. He'll be relentless to catch me now."

Wyatt's jaw tensed, a muscle moving there. He returned his gaze to the fire. "I remember the deal."

When I struck the deal with Prince Lark, Wyatt had yelled at me. He had rebelled and not talked to me for a few days. Until then, we had been close, almost like best friends, but after the deal, Wyatt distanced himself from me.

My head wondered why, but my heart knew the answer.

I flexed my fingers, noticing I was feeling rested, though my muscles were still sore from the whole ordeal. I reached for my socks and pants and pulled them underneath the blankets. When I had them zipped up, I pushed the blankets away and stood.

"I should get going," I said, shoving my feet into my boots.

Wyatt stood, hard eyes on me. "Where are you going?"

"It doesn't matter." I shrugged. "More shadow fae will show up soon, and I can't be here."

Something in my chest constricted. I had just rescued Farrah from the shadow fae. I had just found her after so many agonizing years.

"I'm going with you," I blurted out before I could even make a real decision.

Farrah froze, her sapphire eyes wide. "You? Why? No!"

I suppressed a wince, but I was sure she saw it. What did she want me to do, then? Just let her go knowing she was running for her life? For her fucking freedom?

I had purposely made myself scarce and put distance between us. But here she was, right in front of me, beautiful and angelic as ever with her long silver hair, her bright blue eyes, her smooth skin, and her long, lean body. A deep feeling, something raw, stirred inside my chest—a desperate need, a mad desire. From the moment I met her years, I had felt attracted to her. Then I got to know her and I fell for her. Back then, she was a beautiful girl. Now she was a stunning woman. It was hard to peel my eyes off her, to control my hands which twitched, wanting to reach to her, to keep my feelings at bay.

Wasn't this fate? Wasn't I meant to help her?

"You were almost caught." I gestured to the mouth of the cave. "If I hadn't randomly found you, you would have —" I pressed my mouth shut, unwilling to say the words. I *loathed* the idea of Farrah becoming that evil prince's bride. "You need my help."

She lifted her delicate chin, brave. "I managed well these past three years. I can take care of myself."

"I know you can, but it'll be even better if I help." I had no idea why I was insisting on this idea, but I couldn't just let her go. Not again.

Farrah shook her head. "No, Wyatt. It's too dangerous."

"The more reason for me to join you," I snapped, my voice rising. My temper flared, but I pushed it back. She couldn't see the crazy motherfucker I had become. If she did, she would never let me stay by her side. And I needed to stay by her side. "Farrah, please."

She shut her eyes for a moment. When she looked at me again, her blue gaze was sorrowful. "All right. But only just I'm far away from here and safe. Then you'll leave."

"Deal." From what I could see, getting far from here and making her safe wouldn't be an easy task, which meant I would spend a long time with her. Until then, I could make her change her mind.

Or not.

Maybe I should just do that and really leave. She didn't need me around to taint her.

"All right," she said, picking up her leather bag from the ground. With a knot between her brows, she looked around. "Do you need to pack or … ?"

I scurried around the cave, shoving some clothes into a duffel bag, and some snacks and canned food. I didn't have much, never had, and I wouldn't need much in the future, I was sure.

I put on my thick jacket, a wool beanie over my shaggy hair, slung the duffel bag over my shoulder. "I'm ready."

Farrah wiggled her fingers toward the fire. Ice crawled from underneath and doused out the remainder of the fire. "Then, let's go."

FARRAH

WYATT LIKED MY PLAN OF GOING TO EUROPE, BUT HE DIDN'T have a passport. The new idea was to go to Washington state, find someone to make a fake passport for Wyatt, and go to Alaska. From there, we flew to Europe.

But we couldn't walk all to the way to Washington or Alaska, so we stopped by the nearest town and borrowed a car. I didn't like doing that, but it wasn't like we had enough money to buy one. I promised myself I would make sure we switched cars every day. This way, the owner could find his stolen car, and we wouldn't be caught by the police.

For hours, Wyatt drove us across Montana toward the west. And for all of those hours, we didn't say anything.

Besides still sore, I now felt restless and tense, as if I had to break the ice somehow.

"Hm, have you heard from Luana or Keeran?" I finally asked, glad I could think of a neutral topic to talk about.

Eyes on the road, Wyatt shook his head once. "I haven't spoken or heard of them since I left."

"You've been alone all of this time?" My heart hurt for him. I had been alone because I had to, but he could have stayed with them. Or he could have looked for another pack.

"Not completely," he said, his voice low. "I had a good friend, a half-demon called Rey. Last I heard, he had become a professor in an academy for demon hunters. The Blackthorn Hunters Academy. But that was a while ago."

I frowned. "Wait. Rey? I know a demon hunter called Rey. He was with—"

"Erin," he finished for me. He turned big eyes at me, then fixed on the road again. "You met Rey and Erin?"

"Yeah, and there was another one with them, Harvey."

"I don't know any Harvey, but I do know Rey and Erin," he said. "Rey and I were good friends, and Erin crashed at my place once."

I gawked at him. "What a small world."

"I'll say," he muttered. "How did you meet them?"

"Guess," I said with a sarcastic tone. "I was running from the shadow fae. I hid in a small town in Colorado, and they burned it to the ground to draw me out. That brought demon hunters to the scene. The demon hunters would have killed me too, if it weren't for Rey, Erin, and Harvey."

"I'm glad they helped you." Wyatt tapped his thumb on the wheel. "Demon hunters don't take well to any kind of supernaturals."

"Then I'm lucky," I whispered.

After a moment of silence, Wyatt asked, "What about you? Have you talked to Luana and Keeran?"

I glanced out the window, to the snow-covered fields lining the road. "No. I had to be alone so I could hide, but Daleigh managed to find me a couple of times." Which still bogged my mind. How did my brother manage it? I knew he was a good tracker, always had been, but finding me in the middle of nowhere? That was something.

We fell silent again, the air thick around us.

I tried thinking of other topics to talk about, just so I didn't feel so uncomfortable in this car, but Wyatt spoke up before I could come up with anything.

"Tell about the fae," Wyatt said, his eyes still on the road. "I know you're Frost fae, and there's the Shadow fae, but there are more, aren't there?"

"Yes." Glad we have found a new subject to talk about, I shifted in my seat, adjusting my weight. "There are a bunch of kinds, but the main are Frost, Shadow, Light, and Blaze. The fae king is a Shadow fae, and his son, Prince Lark, was sent to Earth to watch out for the fae who were banished here."

"Why were you banished?"

I frowned, a little taken back by his directness. I let out a long sigh, deciding to tell him the truth. "It was Daleigh's fault. He came to Earth to do some work for the Fae King, and fell in love with a human. He couldn't stay here, so he brought her to the Fae Realm. Such thing is forbidden. Daleigh tried to keep her hidden, but of course she was found out. The Fae King had her killed and banished most of the Frost fae to the human realm as a punishment."

"There's no way to go back?"

I shook my head, even though he was looking at the road. "No. They took our medallions, the ones that could open the portal to takes us back. I haven't seen one in ... I don't even know how long." I glanced at my hands, imagining my magic running inside my veins. "The problem is, we can't survive for long outside the fae realm. It has been too long already."

This time, he glanced at me. "What do you mean?"

"First, our powers fade, and later, our bodies slow down, until we also fade away," I said in a low voice. "We don't know for certain how many more years, or months we have left, but I'm sure soon, we'll see our magic leaving us. In fact, the few frost fae who were born here were born without any magic."

Wyatt gripped the wheel tight, his knuckles turning white. "Then we have to find a way to take you all back."

"The only way right now is for me to give in to Prince Lark," I muttered. "If I marry him, he'll end our banishment and my people will be welcomed back into the Fae Realm."

"How do you know that? That wasn't part of the deal when we took the dagger?"

"Prince Lark promised that to Daleigh in one of their talks."

A muscle tensed in his neck. "Fuck, no, there has to be another way."

I snorted, amused. As if Daleigh and I, and everyone else, hadn't thought of all the possible ways. Unless we found a medallion, stole it, and used it. But even then, we would have to live in hiding since we hadn't been welcomed back, and hiding an entire tribe in the fae realm would be too damn hard.

I shifted my eyes to the snow-covered trees outside, not willing to argue about this matter. Daleigh and I had already argued to last a century. My poor brother felt terrible for what he had done to our people and I knew he would do anything to correct his mistake.

Even to hand out his sister to an evil prince.

It wasn't the first time he had handed me to evil beings, after all.

Wyatt didn't ask any more questions as we drove along the highway. Hours later, we stopped in a small town and found a small inn just outside the town's limit.

Wyatt went in to get us rooms, and he came back a moment, a deep frown in between his brows.

"What is it?" I asked, exiting the car.

Wyatt lifted the keycard in his hand. "There's only one room."

I swallowed. Being in the same bedroom as Wyatt would be even tenser than being inside the car for so long. But I put on a nonchalant mask and shrugged. "It's okay." At least, in case of danger, we would be together.

We picked our bags and went back inside. The inn was as uncared for and ugly on the inside as it was on the outside. Fraying dark green carpet, a wooden desk in desperate need of repair, furniture that was probably from two centuries ago. I wouldn't dare sit on that nasty looking couch. Besides looking filthy, it would probably break under my weight.

Wyatt and I took the stairs to the second floor where a long corridor with the same dark green corridor and terrible flowery wallpaper greeted us. Our bedroom was right at the end of the corridor, near the emergency exit. Good, in case we needed to run in the middle of the night. I hoped we didn't have to, but there had been way too many times when I thought I was well hidden and I had been found out.

Wyatt ran the keycard on the card reader and the green light turned on. He pushed the door open and stepped aside, letting me in first. I took two steps and halted.

"Hm." I pressed my lips, my eyes on the queen bed in the middle of the room. The only bed.

"Oh." Wyatt stood behind me, looking at the bed over my head. "I thought ..." He shook his head and walked past me. "It's okay. I've been sleeping in a cave for the past couple of years. I'm fine sleeping on the floor."

He set his bag down and opened the only closet in the room. He pulled out a folded blanket from it and spread it on the floor, at the bed's feet.

I frowned but didn't object.

Until we were ready to lie down and turn off the lights.

I stood beside the bed, watching as Wyatt sat down on the blanket. Something flared inside me.

"All right," I said, letting out a long breath. "Come over here."

Wyatt turned wary eyes at me. "What?"

"I know you're a werewolf, Wyatt, but you're not a dog. Just because you were sleeping on a cave, doesn't mean you have to sleep on the floor now." I patted the mattress beside me. "The bed is big enough for both of us."

His brows hiked up. "No, it's fine."

"It's not fine with me." I stared at him, unrelenting.

After a quiet heartbeat, Wyatt stood and walked to the other side of the bed. Though my insides tightened at the thought of him so close to me, I hopped into the bed as if this was the most normal thing. Slowly, Wyatt sat down beside me. I lay down, fluffing my pillow under my head.

Wyatt turned off the lights and lay back beside me.

I could feel the heat radiating from his body, I could hear his breathing faster than it should be. And he probably could hear my heartbeat, even faster.

I closed my eyes. This was okay, I told myself. It was just Wyatt. We had spent so much time with each other, we had fought together, I had seen him at his worst after Soren's spell broke and he had to live with the memories of all the terrible things he had done. I had been there, helping him, holding him together.

There was a new darkness in him. He was quiet and reserved, and he barely looked me in the eyes, as if he didn't want me to see what he was hiding inside. But for some reason, I wanted to see. I wanted to know.

I turned to my side and faced him.

Still on his back, Wyatt turned his head and looked at me. "What? Something wrong?"

"Well, lots of things are wrong," I started. "But I want to know about you. How are you doing?"

Wyatt twisted, laying on his side, his whole body mirroring mine. "Right now, I'm trying to sleep."

One corner of my lips turned up. "How's that going for you?"

He snorted. "Great."

I watched his silhouette in the dark, barely making out the features of his face. "Why do you want to come with me, Wyatt?" I asked the question that had been burning in my mind since he first insisted on joining me.

He inhaled deeply, his chest expanding, and the line of his shoulders moving against the faint glow spilling from below the closed curtains. "I just—"

He clamped his mouth.

Oh, not fair. "Come on, say it."

"Shhh," he said, sitting up. Wyatt closed his eyes and focused, probably hearing something I couldn't.

"What is it?" I whispered, pushing up to sit beside him.

He opened his eyes and looked at me, half his face shrouded by the darkness. "We're not alone."

6

WYATT

THE SLOW, QUIET FOOTSTEPS STOPPED IN FRONT OF THE bedroom's door. The person inhaled deeply.

I jumped off the bed, quickly took off my shirt and pants, and transformed into a wolf. A moment later, Farrah was by my side, her hands up, her magic ready at her fingers.

A crackling sound came from the door as something spread over its surface. Ice.

"Who—?" I didn't get to finish my sentence as the door flew open and a man stepped forward into the dark room. Who the fuck cared who it was? It was an intruder and that was all I needed to know.

I pounced on the man.

A blast of ice shot through the air. I was able to push my weight to the side and avoid being hit by one centimeter. But I landed right at the intruder's feet. I bared my teeth.

"No!" Farrah shouted. She stepped in between the stranger and me and pushed us both back. "Wyatt, it's Daleigh."

Fuck, it was her brother. I stepped back until I was behind the bed. Still in the dark, I changed back into my human form and shoved my pants back. Then I turned on the side lamps.

Daleigh stood in front of Farrah, his icy blue eyes murderous. "You're running. Again."

"I thought you had understood that I will always run," Farrah said. "No matter what you say, I won't go with you."

Daleigh pressed the bridge of his nose. "Farrah ..."

"Don't Farrah me," she hissed.

I marched to them and stood beside her. I pointed to Daleigh's chest. "It's your fucking mess, dude, and you're trying to get your sister to fix it for you? Man up and fix it yourself."

Daleigh turned his deadly gaze to me before looking at his sister again. "You told him," he said through gritted teeth.

Farrah lifted her chin. "What if I did?"

Daleigh shook his head, his eyes still on Farrah. "Stay out of this, Wyatt. It doesn't concern you."

Of course, it concerned me. Everything about Farrah concerned me.

"Leave, Daleigh." Farrah gestured to the door behind us. "Pretend you haven't seen me."

"You know I can't do that," Daleigh said. "You know

what I said would happen if you didn't come on your own."

I frowned. What did he say?

Farrah took a step back. "If you try taking me by force, I'll fight you."

I stared at them. What the fuck? He was going to take her by force? Over my dead body. I stepped in front of Farrah. "You better go, Daleigh." I leaned closer to him. Daleigh was as tall as I was, but I was wider than he was. In a fight with strength, I had no doubts I would win. But he had powerful magic. I had to be careful. Still, I bared my teeth and threatened him. "Try to take her and I'll rip out your throat."

"Wyatt!" Farrah snapped.

Sure, he was her brother, but right now, he was being a motherfucker.

Ice formed over Daleigh's hand. "I'm not afraid of you."

He got ready to shoot at me and I prepared myself to shift.

A thick wall of ice appeared between us. "Stop, both of you." Farrah grabbed my arm and pulled me away from the ice. "Daleigh, I won't go with you, no matter what you do. If you try taking me by force, I'll kill myself."

My head snapped toward Farrah. What the fuck?

"Farrah," Daleigh muttered from the other side of the wall. "Please."

"Go," she said, her voice louder.

Daleigh stood still behind the wall for a few seconds, but finally, he let out a long breath and marched away from the bedroom. I closed my eyes and focused on his footsteps, until they left the building and I couldn't hear them anymore.

"He's gone," I said, opening my eyes. Farrah exhaled, her shoulders sagging. My fingers twitched to hold her. "Are you okay?"

She snorted. "My own brother wants to drag me to an evil prince. Does that sound okay to you?"

I stepped closer to her and rested my hands on her shoulders, holding her firmly. My eyes on hers, I made a promise to her. "I won't let him take you."

She stared at me for a few seconds, her sapphire eyes shining in the dark. "I believe you."

An urge to pull her to me, to wrap my arms around her, to bury my face into her hair, hit me right in the chest.

Instead, I dropped my hands.

With a sigh, Farrah picked up her bag and turned to the bed. "We need to go."

7

FARRAH

My frustration with Daleigh only grew as Wyatt and I went to get our borrowed car from the parking lot and found it disabled. Daleigh had made a hole in the fuel tank and all the fuel had leaked out. When we checked the other few cars on the parking lot, we found they were all in the same situation.

In the cold and dark of the night, Wyatt and I had to walk back into the town and steal another car.

Then we drove away.

After a few minutes, my adrenaline and rage seeped out of me and I surrendered to the warmth of the car and its lulling movement. When I woke up, the sun was rising on the horizon.

Behind the wheel, Wyatt rolled his shoulders and neck.

"We can switch," I offered, sitting straighter. "I can drive for a bit so you can sleep."

"No, it's okay," he said, his attention on the road. "I like to drive."

So I let him, but I kept my eyes on him. The last thing we needed was for us to be involved in an accident.

We drove mostly in silence for the most part of the day, stopping just a couple of times for bathroom breaks and food.

The sun was dipping down behind the scenery when we finally made into the border between the United States and Canada.

Wyatt and I stopped the car along the road, a mile from the border.

"I don't have a passport to cross," Wyatt reminded me.

"We could still find a place to make you a fake one," I said, watching as a few cars drove by, going toward the border.

"Or ... I can shift." He turned his hazel eyes to me. The shine of the sunset illuminated his face, giving him a sun-kissed glow. "And you can glamour yourself on top of me so you won't be seen. The border guards will think I'm just a lost wolf."

I frowned. I didn't know much about the wildlife around this side of the country. Were wolves common around here? If not, seeing a wolf crossing the border would raise some alarms, but not the kind that would get us arrested.

It was a valid plan.

So, Wyatt and I waited until the sun was completely

gone and it was fully dark outside before stepping out of the car and putting our plan in motion. With my back to him, Wyatt stripped off his clothes and shifted into a werewolf. If he was cold, he didn't complain. I hoped the fur was enough to keep him warm. I strapped our bags across my shoulders and very gently sat on top of him. I knew I wasn't too heavy, but with the bags, it could get to a considerate weight, especially for a wolf that hadn't been created to be ridden.

Wyatt let out a low bark, letting me know he was ready.

I inhaled deeply, calling on my magic. The glamour fell over me like a cloak, enveloping me and the bags. To anyone who looked at us, all they would see was a huge brown wolf.

"I'm ready," I told him, holding on to his neck gently.

Wyatt started moving, slowly at first, but as he approached the border wall beside the customs checkpoint, he sped up.

The officers saw us, and the people in the cars too. They all pointed to the wolf. Some families returned to the cars, afraid of Wyatt, and while some officers stepped back, others lifted their rifles toward us.

My heart skipped a beat. Wyatt sped up some more, and I had to hold on tighter, even though I was afraid of hurting him.

But the officers didn't shoot. They just watched us until we were way past their sight. Wyatt didn't slow down, though, not until we encountered the first town.

Then, behind a gas station, he shifted back into his human.

"For a moment there, I thought they were going to shoot," he said after he was dressed again.

"Me too," I confessed, still feeling a little on the edge, remembering the gun pointed at us.

"But it worked," he said with a slight smile. "We're here."

I smiled back.

Together, Wyatt and I entered the gas station store and bought some food and drinks. Then we stared out the window.

"We need to steal one again," I muttered, not liking that.

"I know." Wyatt gave me his Gatorade bottle. "Go to the entrance of the gas station. If you want, you can even start walking away. I'll meet you there with our new car."

I wanted to tell him I would help him, but I knew that it would be probably quieter and faster if one of us stole the car alone. So I nodded, and with our things, I marched away from the gas station.

The snow crunched under my soles, my boots sinking into the fluffy white. Though it was probably too cold for Wyatt, I enjoyed the chill breeze blowing over my face. I stretched my neck, relishing in the sensation. It felt like batteries recharging my powers.

A few minutes passed. I bit the inside of my cheek as I gained distance from the gas station. Where was Wyatt? Was he caught? With that in mind, I stopped and looked back. Should I go back and check it out? No, I would give him a few more minutes.

Worried, I gave him just one more minute then started my way back, just as the sound of wheels squealing echoed through the white landscape and a blue truck sped my way.

I stepped back as the truck stopped by my side.

"Get in!" Wyatt shouted, opening the passenger door for me.

I jumped into the truck and slammed the door. "Couldn't you get something less conspicuous?"

"It was the easiest one to steal," he said, his gaze divided between the road ahead of us and the rearview mirror.

I glanced back. "Is there someone following us?"

"They might come if they are fast enough." At that, Wyatt sped up.

I kept an eye on the road behind us, but if someone came, they were too late.

Wyatt and I drove for a couple of hours, well into the night, and again I kept an eye on him. We hadn't slept properly in a couple of days now. Soon, he would pass out of exhaustion.

Around three in the morning, I urged him to stop. "Just find a side road, pull over, and let's sleep for a little while."

He glanced at me for a second, a frown between his brows, before returning his gaze to the road. "I don't like just stopping anywhere, but you're right. We need to rest."

It didn't take long for us to find a smaller road. Wyatt

turned into it. He drove for about a mile, just so the truck wasn't visible from the main road, but as he pulled over, the truck's lights illuminated the broken gates just ahead of us.

Past the gates, sat a big ranch like house, but with its open door, broken windows, and peeling paint, it was clearly abandoned.

"We can sleep in there," I suggested, seeing a chimney peeking from the roof. "Maybe we can even make a fire."

I didn't have to tell Wyatt twice. He pushed open the broken gate and drove through the snow until the side of the ranch, where he parked the truck—from here, it wouldn't be seen from the road. To make things even less undisturbed, I used my powers to smooth out the snow, erasing the wheels' marks from the snow.

Together, we entered the house through the broken front door. My hand immediately flew to the light switch, and to my surprise, the lights on the foyer turned on. Though the immediate rooms were empty and dusty, the interior of the house seemed intact—the doors and windows closed all the way, and some even had a couple of pieces of furniture. Past the foyer and the living room, there was a sitting room with a fireplace, a dining room, a study of sorts, a half bath, and a kitchen. The stairs leading to the second floor were located at the foyer, but since we had all we needed down here, we didn't even check the second floor out.

Wyatt knelt in front of the fireplace and worked on

cleaning it up, while I checked our bags for blankets. The cold didn't bother me, but I knew Wyatt with his hot werewolf blood had to be feeling it.

After a few tries, Wyatt was able to light the fireplace with the little firewood it had.

He smiled at me. "Finally."

After turning off the lights, I spread one of our blankets right in front of the fireplace and we sat on it. If we were really careful, we wouldn't have any lights on or turned on the fireplace, but since the house didn't seem to have a working central air, we opted for the fireplace. Hopefully, the house was far from the main road and no one would see the smoke rising from the chimney.

Wyatt sat beside me, both of us staring as the fire took life and started warming the sitting room.

"Farrah," Wyatt started after a while in silence.

"Hm," I said, feeling sleepy. We really should get some shut-eye tonight. We needed it. I hugged my knees and rested my head over them.

"I just wanted you to know ..." He turned his head to me, his hazel eyes shining with the fire light. "I won't let anything happen to you. I'll protect you, even if it's from Daleigh himself."

A small smile tugged at my lips. "Thanks."

"I mean it." He reached over and placed his hand over mine. "If you allow me, I'll be by your side." He paused, his eyes intent on mine. "Always."

I stilled.

We had talked about this. Well, sort of. I had told him he could help me escape, but that was it. I couldn't be with him for long. It wouldn't be fair, for him and for me.

"Please, don't," I whispered.

"I don't know what you're afraid of, but I don't care." He took my hand in his, making me loose the grip on my knees. "I'm just glad I found you again."

"I'm glad I found you too, but whatever you're imagining, it can't happen, Wyatt." I gently extricated my hand from his. Damn it, I didn't want to have this conversation. I didn't want to hurt his feelings.

His brows curled down. "I know I'm not good enough for you, but—"

"That's not it," I cut him off before he said something stupid. Not good for me? Wyatt was the best thing that had happened in my life in years.

"Then what is it?" Wyatt opened his mouth again, but closed it a moment later, his eyes wide. He placed a hand over his lips. "Shh."

God damn it, again?

Slowly, a figure appeared from the shadows of the room. Because of the darkness and the weak fire light, the only thing I could make out was that it was human shaped.

"Who's there?" I asked, standing up and channeling my power.

Wyatt jumped to his feet beside me, ready to turn into his wolf self.

"You're not welcome here," an eerie voice echoed through the room. "Leave this place."

"We mean no harm," I said, hoping I didn't look too threatening. "We just want shelter for the night."

The figure took a few steps forward, revealing a lean woman with long, blond curls. "Who are you and what are you doing here?"

8

WYATT

"You first," I said, ready to shift and attack this woman if she as much as looked the wrong way.

She stared at us, her gray-blue eyes shining like stone gems in the dim light. "My name is Ariella, and I'm an angel."

I frowned. Angel? Never heard of that one before.

I took her in. She did look angelic with her too white skin, her bright eyes, and her long white-blond curls. Though the jeans pants, the beige sweater, and the brown boots didn't really scream angel to me.

Beside me, Farrah took a sharp inhale. "Ariella, I'm Farrah, a Frost fae, and this is Wyatt, a werewolf," she explained, her voice gentle and almost reverent. What the fuck? "We're hiding here for the night, running from the fae who are forcing me to marry Prince Lark, the Shadow fae prince."

"A forced marriage?" Ariella shook her head, her curls bouncing side to side. "That's not good."

"We're trying to get to Alaska so we can hide for a while, before moving on to Europe," Farrah continued, detailing our entire plan to this stranger.

I stared at her, incredulous. "Why the fuck are you telling her all of this?"

"She's an angel," Farrah whispered, as if I didn't know what an angel was. "Angels are divine creatures." I didn't believe in the divine, or even evil. Everything was a choice. "Stay quiet. Angels usually don't like werewolves. Or vampires, witches, etc."

Oh, that was fucking perfect.

"I see," Ariella said, her tone flat. I wondered if her powers included enhanced hearing and if she had heard us. She turned her eyes to me, her nose wrinkled. "I'll allow you to stay, werewolf, because you're protecting a fae. You two can spend the night here."

Farrah smiled at the angel. "Thank you."

Ariella retreated to the shadows and a moment later, she was gone.

Without any ceremonies, Farrah sat back down on the blanket.

"How can you relax knowing there's a stranger in this house?" I asked, looking around, expecting Ariella to jump from a corner and attack us. It didn't matter if she was an angel and supposedly divine. She was a stranger to us. We didn't know her story. She could have chosen evil long ago.

"Nothing will happen, Wyatt." Farrah tugged at the hem of my pants. "Sit down and relax."

My eyes in the shadows, I sat down, but I didn't relax.

Soon, Farrah lay at my side and fell asleep, but I couldn't.

I stayed up the entire night.

***

IT WAS EARLY MORNING WHEN FARRAH FINALLY WOKE UP. During the night, I had debated waking her up several times, wanting to bolt before it was too late. But she had been sleeping so peacefully after so many nights on the run. I couldn't do that to her.

Looking chipper than usual, Farrah practically skipped to the bathroom, where she washed up. And I was fucking ready to leave this place.

I started packing.

And Ariella came back.

Tension rolling in waves through my body, I stood, facing her.

"Relax, werewolf," Ariella said. "I won't hurt you."

Farrah came out of the bathroom and smiled at the angel. "Good morning."

Ariella returned the smile, though it was a small one. "Morning." She glanced at the bags at my feet. "Ready to go?"

"Yes," I said, eager to leave this place.

"I'll go with you," Ariella announced.

I stared at her. What the fuck?

"That's good," Farrah said. "We could use more help."

I snapped my head to Farrah. More help? She didn't even want mine to begin with. Now she was letting an angel tag along just like that?

My temper rose pretty quickly.

Ariella walked out of the house, and I turned to Farrah. "How are you so ...?" I didn't even know a word for it. Relaxed? Okay? Content?

"She's an angel, Wyatt," Farrah said, as if that was explanation enough. "Angels are inherently good. She won't be able to hurt us without betraying who she is. That's why she wants to help, because it's in her nature."

"Everyone can change," I said, my jaw tense. "I bet even angels."

Farrah rested a hand on my chest. "Don't worry. We're two. If for some reason she moves the wrong way, we can take her."

I knew that, but why risk it?

Still, when Farrah looked at me with those bright blue eyes, her face calmer than I had seen in years, I knew I wouldn't be able to argue anymore. She was the only one who could disarm me with one single glance.

I exhaled deeply. "All right."

And like a fool, I followed her out.

9

FARRAH

Wᴙᴀᴛᴛ ʜᴇʟᴅ ᴛʜᴇ ᴛʀᴜᴄᴋ'ꜱ ᴡʜᴇᴇʟ ᴡɪᴛʜ ᴀ ᴅᴇᴀᴛʜ ɢʀɪᴘ ᴀꜱ ʜᴇ drove us away from the ranch.

After a few tense minutes, I twisted on the passenger seat so I could look at Ariella seated on the back.

"So, Ariella," I started, careful. "It's uncommon to find angels in the middle of nowhere, and alone. May I ask what happened to you?"

Ariella's glanced out the window, to the impossibly white landscape as the sun rose somewhere behind a mountain. I thought she wouldn't answer it and was about to apologize for asking when she returned her eyes to me, a sad glint on them.

"Long ago, I came down for a mission with my team," she started, her voice low. "We hadn't been on Earth for two days when demons found us. Higher level demons. They set up a trap and we fell on it like idiots." She swallowed hard. "The demons killed my entire team. I was hurt, but I managed to escape, though, while I fought my way out, the demons ripped out my wings."

I gasped. Holy shit, wings were everything for an angel. "I'm so sorry."

She nodded as she continued, "I can't go back without my wings. After I recovered, I went after the demons, but I couldn't find them. I've searched for them for many years, but a couple of months ago, I lost their tracks completely." She looked down at her hands. "So, I hid in that house, ashamed of myself."

"It wasn't your fault," I told her.

"It may not be, but I still feel guilty for all that happened." She shifted her eyes to the truck's window again.

Survivor's guilt. I had heard that was a real thing. Besides that, Ariella had lost the one thing that could take her home and marked her as an angel: her wings. Without them, she wasn't only lost.

She was a fallen angel.

If she hadn't said those words out loud, she was either in denial, or she didn't want to tell us that. But I knew enough of angels to know that was a real thing. Now, Wyatt's fears could be reasoned with, since fallen angels could indeed turn evil.

Slowly, I sat straight again, and try to organize my thoughts as Wyatt drove on. Ariella couldn't be evil. If she were, she would have attacked us when we were alone in that house. She wouldn't have even introduced herself. She would have simply pounced on us while we sleep and killed us.

No, she wasn't evil. She had a sad and wistful air over her, but there wasn't anything devious or dark.

I wished that somehow, we could help her. If she had her wings, she would come into her full powers and go back home. But our plates were already too full. We couldn't handle helping others at the moment.

For the next hour, silence reigned in the truck. When we couldn't take anymore, Wyatt relented and stopped the truck beside a snow ditch just outside the road, a few yards away from a gas station. With my powers, I made the snow ditch bigger, just so no one could see the truck, no matter what way they came, then we went to the gas station's store where we bought some food and ate breakfast at the counter along the window.

All in silence.

I was dying to break the ice between Wyatt and Ariella, but I wasn't sure how to do that. Angels hated any other supernaturals except for fae, and Wyatt didn't seem to trust anyone right now.

After we ate, we walked back to the truck.

Just outside the gas station, Wyatt halted, his eyes alert.

I groaned. "Don't tell me."

"Shh," he said, straining to hear whatever he was hearing.

But I didn't need to wonder about it. Half a second later, the world exploded into ice and snow as frost fae surrounded us.

Without hesitation, Wyatt shifted into a werewolf and I called on my magic. But before I could attack, Ariella grabbed my arms and pulled me back.

"Let me go," I hissed. "I need to fight."

"They are here to take you," Ariella said. "You need to run."

Yes, I needed to run, but not without Wyatt. I jerked against Ariella's tight grip, but she didn't let go. Were angels stronger than fae and I didn't remember? Damn it!

In the growing distance, I saw as the frost fae warriors created an ice cage around Wyatt, trapping him. Wyatt snarled from the cage as Daleigh stepped away from the warriors, revealing himself. Daleigh's lips moved, but I couldn't hear what he was saying.

That was it. This angel be damned.

I froze the skin of my arms, so cold, it burned Ariella's hands with frostbite. She yelped and dropped her hands. I didn't think twice. I just ran toward Wyatt.

Until something hit me from behind, a magical force that pushed me down on the snow and slowly spread over my body. I blinked trying to fight the pain and dizziness overtaking me.

"I'm sorry," I heard as a pair of feet appeared right beside my head.

Then I went under.

10

DALEIGH, THE MOTHERFUCKER, LET HIS FROST FAE WARRIORS beat me up before taking me deeper into the woods, where the snow came up to their chests. In a large clearing, they used the magic to melt the snow, and placed my ice cage right in the center. More frost fae arrived and all twenty of them formed a wide circle around the clearing, just waiting.

Since Daleigh wasn't able to get Farrah, he took me as bait.

This was a trap for her.

Hurt and bleeding, I had rammed into this fucking cage several times, but it was magically reinforced. I couldn't break the ice with my weakened brute force.

With his superior air stamped on his face, Daleigh approached the cage and threw in a pair of pants and a heavy coat. "Change if you want. Or remain as a wolf, I don't really care."

I eyed the clothing pieces at my paws. What was he playing at?

With all their backs to me, I shifted into my human form and quickly dressed in the pants and coat. I really could use some thick socks and a sweater right now, but I wouldn't tell him that. Instead, I focused on the heat from my werewolf and called it within me. I could keep myself from freezing in this fucking weather for a little while.

Since I didn't have any first aid kit, I scooped snow from the ground and pressed it to my wounds, hoping it would help with swelling and stop the bleeding. They had been careful not to do any permanent damage, just enough to cripple me so I couldn't fight back.

Even though I wished he stayed away from me, Daleigh came back and stood just a few feet from the cage.

"Tell me, what do you think you're doing?"

"You mean, protecting your sister so she doesn't end up in a forced marriage with an evil fae?" I asked, my voice full of disdain.

"You're not protecting her," he said, his icy eyes hard on mine. "You're adding to her pain."

I frowned. "By helping her? By loving her?"

Daleigh shook his head. "A fae could never be a wolf."

What the fuck was that supposed to mean?

"If that's some rule from the fae realm, well, I'm glad to say we're not there," I retorted.

"You're so pitiful. You don't even know the consequences of it all if Farrah stays with you."

A wave of rage washed through me. "Just because you

fucked up when you took a human to the fae realm, doesn't mean Farrah will, okay?"

Anger flashed in Daleigh's eyes. It was clear he hated that Farrah had told me about what happened, what he did for his people to be thrown in here against their will.

"It can't work," Daleigh insisted, his voice darker. "It never will. I made a terrible mistake, and now my people are paying. I'll do anything to rectify my mistake."

"Even handing your own sister to an evil prince?" I poked him with an invisible hot iron. "I can see that."

"I won't try to reason with you," Daleigh said, shaking his head. "If you really love Farrah, you will let her go. You will forget about her. That's the best you can do."

I opened my mouth to snap at him again, but the sudden bleak shine on Daleigh's eyes shut me up. For a moment, he looked sad. Before I could make sense of it, or tease him about it, Daleigh spun around and marched away, to stand at the circle around my cage with the rest of the frost fae.

I glared at his back, my mind reeling. What did he mean when he said I didn't know about the consequences of loving Farrah? Was this just another way to get into my head and disarming me?

It didn't matter. Farrah was everything to me. She was my reason for living and I would fight for her no matter the outcome might be.

A COUPLE OF HOURS PASSED, AND I STARTED LOSING THE fight against my injuries. Soon, I would blackout. If I did, then how could I help Farrah when she came? Or better yet, tell her to stay away and run before it was too late?

I thought things couldn't get worse when five more figures arrived at the scene—five fae dressed in black armor and big, fur-lined cloaks.

The Shadow Fae.

And right in the middle of them, was General Auron, Prince Lark's first hand.

Daleigh went to greet him. "I see you've got my message."

General Auron nodded. He glanced at me. If he recognized me from the time Farrah, Luana, and I tried to steal the Dagger of All Hunting from Prince Lark's fortress, he didn't show. "You say she'll come for him?"

"She will," Daleigh assured him. "And when she does, we'll be ready for her."

"Good." General Auron jerked his chin once and the other four Shadow fae spread out through the clearing, taking their places among the frost fae warriors.

Fear mixed with the fury inside of me.

Farrah wouldn't just walk into a trap. She was coming to her end.

11

FARRAH

I WOKE UP IN FRONT OF THE FIREPLACE, A QUIET FIRE sparking amid the cold. What the hell happened? Why was I back at the ranch? I frowned, my mind catching up.

The gas station, the ambush, Wyatt.

With a gasp, I shot to my feet.

"Easy there," a voice said. I turned around and found Ariella seated along the wall on the other side of the room. "You might still feel dizzy." She grabbed a cookie from the plastic package in her hands. "Want one?"

Dim light streamed through the window. It was already sunset, which meant, I had been passed out for hours.

I stared at her, dumbfounded. "What did you do?"

"I saved you." She shoved the cookie in her mouth.

"No, you doomed Wyatt."

Chewing, Ariella stood up. After she swallowed, she said, "If I hadn't taken you, Wyatt would have been killed and you would have been taken. All I did was buy you some time."

My anger didn't lessen, but maybe she had a point. "Live to fight another day."

"Well, honestly, that wasn't my first intention when I saved you," Ariella confessed. "After all, he is a werewolf. I couldn't care less about his life." She grabbed another cookie from the package. "Why don't you forget about him and take advantage that the fae are distracted with him to run away? This would be the perfect opportunity to get very far away from them."

She was right, but that didn't sit right with me. How could I leave Wyatt behind? He meant to me more than I could ever say out loud. Even if in the end we couldn't be together, I wouldn't let him be a beating sack to Daleigh and his warriors. Besides, I knew that if I didn't show up, they wouldn't let Wyatt go. They would kill him.

I would never be okay with that.

"I don't care," I told her. "I'm going after him."

"I knew you would say that." A white light flashed from Ariella's hand. I blinked in surprise as I dodged the hit. She was trying to strike me again.

Enraged, I quickly brought an ice wall around her, purposely bringing it up to her chin and trapping her hands inside. "I understand if you don't want to help me. But you can't stop me either." I took a step back. "Just stay here and continue living the way you were living. I don't care. Just … if you won't help, then leave us alone."

Without another glance at the fallen angel, I turned around and ran out of the house.

As I suspected, Daleigh didn't try to hide. He made sure I had tracks to follow from where they attacked us to the place where they held Wyatt.

Even under the faint moonlight, I could see the tracks easily. I was anxious at first, eager to get this done and continue running, but when I got there and hid behind the snow and tree trunks, spying out at the clearing, my heart sank.

One, Wyatt was hurt, laying inside the ice cage in the center of the clearing. Two, General Auron was here with another four shadow fae.

Damn it. Daleigh didn't like to waste time. He didn't want to just capture me. He already wanted to hand me out to Prince Lark and get everything done.

Suddenly, Wyatt's head whipped up and his eyes scanned the area I was hiding. He had smelled me, or heard me, with his werewolf senses.

Even though I couldn't read his thoughts, I just knew he was pissed at me.

It didn't matter. I was here to rescue him, and that was exactly what I was going to do.

12

WYATT

What the fuck was Farrah doing? Did she have a death wish? Or maybe she was as scared of marrying the evil prince as she told me. Regardless, she crept up closer, her gaze intent on the fae around the cage.

She quickly took two fae out, the ones that were more far apart, opening a gap on the circle from where she could sneak in. She kept low to the ground, moving very slowly so not to make a sound, though I was sure the rapid beating of my heart was loud enough for everyone in the clearing to hear.

When she finally reached the cage, I couldn't even yell at her. I glared at her, but she didn't pay me any attention. She simply held on to the ice bars and started working her magic on it.

Meanwhile, my heartbeat sped up some more and I glanced around, keeping an eye on the other fae.

When she finally broke three of the bars, she reached for me, her hands gentle over my arms.

"Are you okay?" she mouthed, her bright eyes worried.

I nodded, though the wound on my side hurt like hell. It was the worst one of all.

Gritting my teeth, I crawled past the broken bars. Careful, Farrah helped me up, and without wasting a second, we started the tense trek back to the edge of the forest.

But with my wound and my exhaustion, we were too slow. Halfway through our escape, two frost fae saw us.

"Stop!" they yelled before charging us.

Then all of the frost and shadow fae turned to us.

"Fuck," I muttered.

With a flicker of her hand, Farrah created a giant ice wall to keep everyone out of the way, but the frost fae easily broke through it. She kept trying to create more walls, one after the other, while we slowly advanced, but in less than twenty seconds, we were surrounded by frost and shadow fae.

General Auron stepped forward and twisted his hands. Shadows appeared from under the snow, twirling around Farrah and me.

The snakes of shadows wrapped around my ankles and wrists, keeping me in place. I gritted my teeth and fought against their hold, but the fucking wound on my side stung. My strength was drained. There was nothing I could do now, only watch as Farrah jerked against the shadows tying around her. She tried shooting ice pelts from her hands, but the shadow ropes pulled her hands down, until she was on all four by my side.

She glanced at me, her eyes wide, shining with fear. "I'm sorry."

She was sorry? I was sorry. If it hadn't been for me, she would have been far away from here already. Fuck, how I wished she had stayed away. I would have found a way to escape, eventually, and I would have met her later.

Now we were both caught.

The shadow fae would take Farrah away, and Daleigh would kill me.

Just then, a bright light cut through the clearing.

I recoiled into myself, momentarily blinded by the light. But something else happened: the shadow ropes faded away.

The light shone brighter, sending flashes out, making it impossible to look up.

A hand hooked under my arm. "Help me here, will you?" I gasped, recognizing Ariella's voice. I started opening my eyes, but shut them down instantly, the light too bright. "But keep your eyes closed."

Grunting against the pain rippling through my middle, I pushed the ground and stood, leaning more than I should on Ariella.

"What did you do?" I asked, trying to listen to the fae around us. Some of them were grunting as if they were hurt, but most of them were absolutely quiet.

"I'm hitting them with more light, so most of them

passed out," she explained. "The ones that didn't are fighting against it."

She could control the light like that? That was fucking great.

"What about Farrah?" I asked, suddenly worried she had hit Farrah by mistake.

"I'm here," Farrah said, taking my other arm.

"I won't be able to keep this light so strong for much longer," Ariella said. "We need to go. Now."

With Ariella guiding us, I braced myself against the pain and ran with them.

Five steps later, Farrah let go of me. "I'll be right back," she said.

My heart raced. "What the fuck are you doing?" I tried spying through under my lashes, but couldn't. "Farrah, come back right now."

"I'm here." She stepped to my side, taking my arm again. "Let's go."

Without a moment to waste, we ran.

A couple of minutes later, Ariella told us we could open our eyes. We were deep into the woods, our feet sinking in the snow. Behind us, the bright light still shone. I glanced back, curious, but couldn't see much through the trees.

Soon, we emerged into the place they first attacked us.

Ariella opened the passenger door of the truck we had stolen the previous day. "Get in."

She didn't have to tell me twice.

Farrah hopped on the backseat, while Ariella ran to the other side and slipped behind the wheel.

I frowned as she started the car. "You know how to drive?"

"I've been here for a while," she said, backing the truck out. "I had to learn to do a lot of things." Then she hit the gas and we zoomed into the road, away from the frost and shadow fae.

"Hm," Farrah started from the backseat. "Ariella, thank you. If you hadn't come back—"

Ariella glared at her from the rearview mirror. "I should have let you two rot." The fallen angel shook her head, clearly exasperated. She turned her glare to me. "I can't believe she went back for you."

"Me neither," I muttered.

"I'll always go back for him," Farrah said, her voice loud and firm, her chin high. "I don't care about the dangers, I'll always come back for you." She stretched her arm forward and placed her hand on my shoulder.

Something burned in the back of my eyes. I blinked several times, telling myself it was the fucking pain. It was finally getting to me now that my body was relaxing.

Even though I was touched for her words and her actions, I would have to talk to Farrah later. She couldn't do that again. She shouldn't. If I was caught and she was too, then it was all for nothing.

I loved her too much to let her throw everything away for me.

13

WE DROVE IN TENSE SILENCE FOR A COUPLE OF HOURS. THE three of us were tired, hungry, and Wyatt was hurt. We needed to stop at the next town to rest, eat, clean Wyatt's wound, and to switch our truck. We had been with this one for almost two days now and hadn't gone too far. Soon, we would be seen with it and we would have a new problem on our tail.

But as Ariella turned into the next town on our path, we noticed shadow fae crawling just outside the town's limit. Some hid among the trees, others patrolled the road like guards on a cross-country border.

Without a word, Ariella turned the truck around and continued on the highway.

We tried stopping by the next town, but it was more of the same.

When Ariella turned the truck around, I couldn't stay

quiet. "I have a feeling they will be crowding all towns around here."

"Then we keep going, until we find one where they aren't," Wyatt said from the passenger seat, his voice faint. His face was paler than before, and his hand clutched his side with too much force.

"What if they have fae from here to the border to Alaska?" I asked, leaning forward on the front seats. "You won't be able to shift and carry me like we did last time hurt. You need medical attention now."

Wyatt glanced at Ariella. "You're an angel. Don't you have healing powers?"

Ariella shook her head, her eyes on the road. "It doesn't work like that," was all she said.

Wyatt turned his hazel eyes to me, the light in them dim. "We'll figure something out. We always do."

Frustrated, I sat back on my seat and fished the golden medallion from my pocket.

When Ariella had used her light to help us escape from Daleigh's trap, I had crawled to the nearest shadow fae and stole his medallion. This was the only way for a fae to cross over to the fae realm.

"I might have an idea," I said, my voice low.

"What is it?" Ariella asked, glancing at me through the rearview mirror.

"We go to the fae realm." I held up the medallion so they could see it. "With this."

Wyatt's eyes bugged. "That's why you stopped when we were leaving. You got one of those."

I nodded. "The frost fae's medallions were taken away when we were banished here, but I knew the shadow fae must carry these all the time. So I snatched one up. Just in case." I smoothed my thumb over the medallion's rugged surface. "Now it might be handy."

"I always wanted to go to the fae realm," Ariella said, her tone lighter than a moment before. "I'm in."

"Wait." Wyatt twisted his torso, so he could look at me better. He winced, probably from the pain on his side, but he tried to hide it. "Let's think this through. We go to the fae realm and what? As far as I know, if a werewolf and an angel are seen there, we'll be killed on the spot."

"Well, a werewolf will," I muttered. "But not an angel. Angels are divine creatures." Even fallen angels. Though they would hold Ariella until they found out if she had turned evil or not.

I was still a little mad with her for trying to keep me from Wyatt, but that didn't make her evil. She had even saved us, when she could have simply just walked away.

"Good to know," Wyatt muttered. "But then what? We get there and continue hiding?"

"Then ... I don't know," I admitted. "I think the first thing we need to worry about it treat your wounds, find some food and shelter. We can plan what happens later, later. At least I have this now." I showed them the medallion again. "If we want to come back, we can, at any time."

Wyatt spun forward, his eyes on the road, though I didn't think he was paying attention to it. He was thinking about this new development.

"Will the fae you stolen the medallion from realize what happened?" he asked.

"Since they don't go to the fae realm and don't use the medallion at all, I think it'll take him a while to notice." It made it easier that he hadn't kept his medallion around his neck like most fae. His was tucked in inside a pocket of his armor. Unless he went rummaging through the pockets, he wouldn't know. "And when he notices it, he'll probably think he misplaced it. At least at first. Until they found out I stole it, you'll be healed." And we could use the medallion to portal directly to Europe, as it was our first plan.

Wyatt let out a long breath. "All right. Let's do it."

I tightened my grip around the medallion and smiled, a sudden eagerness filling my chest.

"So, how does this work?" Ariella asked.

"Pull over," I told her.

A moment later, she stopped the truck on the side of the road. The eagerness spread through my whole body and I jumped off the truck, not being able to sit still. Wyatt dragged himself out of the truck, but stayed close to it, his hand on the closed door for balance, and Ariella jogged around the truck and halted by our side.

I stretched my arm forward, toward the snow, and closed my eyes. My magic filled my veins and ran down my arm, reaching the medallion, feeding it. Activating it.

Opening my eyes, I saw as a white light appeared from the medallion. It shone until it formed an oval wall in front of us.

The portal.

"Come with me," I told them before stepping through the portal.

Energy crackled around me in the second it took to cross between worlds. A moment I was in a snow covered Canada, and the next I was in an expansive green meadow, the warm sun shining down on us. Lush grass covered the ground, tall, twisty trees surrounded us, along with moss covered rocks, and pink and orange flowers. Their sweet scent reached my nose and I inhaled deeply.

"Where are we?" Ariella asked, looking around.

"We're at the Woods Court, near the border with the Frost Court," I told them. I had tried creating a portal directly to my home, but I hadn't been able to. Maybe the fae king had cast some spell to block it. "There's a small village nearby. I can gather supplies to treat your wounds there," I told Wyatt.

His brows slammed down. "Isn't that dangerous?"

It was. "Not if I'm careful."

***

"Ouch." Wyatt flinched.

"Such a baby," I muttered under my breath as I applied a smelly salve to the wound on his side.

I had left Wyatt and Ariella at a small meadow while I snuck into the village. First, I stole a gown and a scarf so I could change and hide my silver-blond hair. If I walked in using human clothes and my hair billowing behind me, I would draw unwanted attention. Then, I went to the apothecary, where I pretended to have an interest in some herbs for bathing. When the shop owner was busy with another customer, I stole the healing salve. On my way out of the village, I also stole a warm loaf of bread that a seller had left at a shop window for cooling.

I hated stealing and promised myself that if I ever had money again, I would pay these fae back, but that was very unlikely.

Back at the meadow, I made Wyatt lift his shirt and sit down on a fallen tree trunk so I could treat him. Thankfully, the wound had stopped bleeding and didn't look infected so far. I cleaned the caked blood from around it, then applied a good amount of salve over it. I ripped a tunic I had stolen and tied it around Wyatt's torso.

"There," I said as I stood from the trunk. "Do you think we can keep going, or do you want to rest some more?"

Wyatt stood before me, his tall frame looming over me. He winced as he lifted his arms and moved them side to side. "It hurts but I'll survive."

"Where are we going?" Ariella asked. She stood a few feet away from us, watching the woods with focused eyes.

"Into the Frost Court," I said. "My village should be deserted. We can get to my old family home and hide there for a while, until we plan our next steps."

Ariella nodded, Wyatt stayed quiet.

We started a slow trek toward the border with the Frost Court. The change in scenery was hard to miss. A shallow stream marked the border dividing Woods and the Frost

Courts. One side was green and lush and warm. The other had leafless trees covered in snow.

I couldn't help but smile at the sight of my kingdom.

We found a patch on the stream where some bigger rocks jutted out from under the water, and we crossed the border. As we stepped our feet on the snow, the chill wind blew past us. Ariella and Wyatt, who had taken out their jackets once we crossed the portal, put them back on. I had taken off mine too, but I waited a little, enjoying the cold air on my skin. This was different than the cold in the human world. Here, the cold was part of the land, of the kingdom. It was magical and powerful.

But even a frost fae could die if left in the extreme cold without a jacket for too long. So I put on my coat before leading them into the snow covered woods.

"This way," I said, trying to absorb everything around me. The snow, the icicles trickling down from the leafless tree branches, the cold breeze that blew by every so often, the white scenery that filled my heart with longing.

This was my kingdom. My home.

I was here, not because I should be, but because I had snuck in. If I were caught, my punishment would be worse than marrying the Shadow Prince.

However, if I did that, if I married him, my people would be able to come home and feel this happiness, this elation I was feeling now.

I wondered if I was making the right decision, or if I was being just selfish.

14

WYATT

Since we crossed the border into the Frost Court, Farrah had a bounce to her step, her shoulders seemed lighter, her expression relaxed. It was like the snow and ice were her water and food and air, and she needed them to live. Before, she was just trying to survive.

As we walked parallel to an icy road, hidden behind the frozen trees that flanked the road, Farrah explained a little more about the fae realm. The fae king, Prince Lark's father, was evil and powerful. Ruthless. He wasn't afraid of killing his enemies, or his subjects, in cold blood if they all didn't follow his rules.

And one of those rules was no other race, supernatural or not, should cross over to the fae realm. Which meant, Ariella and I had to be extra careful not to be caught.

But as we advanced to the heart of the Frost Court, we only saw a couple of frost fae traveling through the road. Each time, we stopped, hid better, and waited for them to pass, and each time, I noticed Farrah's eyes as she drank in the fae, as if she had to hold herself back so she wouldn't sprint to them and talk to them.

"I thought all frost fae had been banished to the human world," Ariella said at one point. We had been walking for hours now.

A few yards ahead of us, Farrah shook her head. "Not all, but most. I know the fae king left a couple of villages intact, to show he was merciful, as he said. But I heard these villages are—or were, I don't know anymore—watched by shadow fae day and night. If anyone misbehaves, they are either killed or banished to the human realm."

"I don't understand," I muttered. "How come such an evil king is on power?"

Farrah shrugged. "I don't really know. He has been in power for so long, and it is said he changed most history books so we all learned he was born as the only fae king to ever rule." She scoffed. "And most fae truly believe that."

"Nobody tried to depose him?" I sure would have tried if I had a king this cruel.

"I heard rumors of people trying to make him step down, or even trying to attack him," Farrah said, her voice low. "But he's too powerful. Nobody ever succeeded."

My mind shot to Luana and Keeran, and even Drake and Thea. When their leaders turned evil, they stepped up and acted. They either defeated or killed their previous leaders and created a better world for their people.

Why couldn't the fae do the same?

As I was getting ready to ask about that, Farrah stopped.

"What is it?"

"There a small village up ahead," she said, spying from behind a frozen tree. "The last one before mine."

I loomed behind Farrah and looked out. The village—a gathering of gray wood houses with snow covered roofs—looked abandoned with the accumulated snow in between the houses, and no one out. Not that I could blame them with this fucking cold.

"I think the residents all moved away," Ariella said from beside us.

"Or they were banished too," I said.

"That can't be." Farrah's brows dipped down. "I knew a couple of fae who lived here and they weren't banished with us." She turned to us. "The village looks abandoned, but just in case ..." She wiggled her fingers in my direction, then Ariella's. "I'm glamouring you to give you silver-blond hair and blue or gray eyes, and to make your clothes less modern. But in case we find someone, don't get too close to them. They might be able to see through the glamour."

Without waiting for a response, Farrah marched past the line of trees and into the village.

Ariella sighed. "I don't know what she wants with this village."

"She's just worried," I said, though I agreed with Ariella. If it was my calling, I would have just walked around it and continued our trek to Farrah's home. I jerked my chin toward Farrah. "Come on."

When we caught up with Farrah, she was already rounding a corner of the first house. As we walked into supposedly the main street in the village, I glanced around. Some houses had open doors, some windows were falling off the hinges, and snow accumulated on the porches. There was no shop, no market, no stands ... well, I wasn't sure how they did that before with all the snow, but now there was barely a path to walk. Our feet sank in packed snow as we advanced into the center of the village.

Then I heard a slow breathing coming from one of the houses. "Farrah," I said, my voice low. I stopped. Farrah turned to me. "In the house to my left." I made a small move with my chin toward the said house. "Someone is inside."

Farrah didn't use subtlety as she trekked over the snow toward the house.

A head full of white hair peeked from behind the slightly open door.

"Hi there," Farrah said, slowing down. "Hm, can you tell me what happened here? Where's everyone?"

The door opened a little more and an old female fae stepped under the doorway, half her body still hidden. She looked scared, wary. "Don't you know?"

Farrah shook her head. "No. I've been away for too long."

The old fae took a step forward and glanced side to side, as if looking out for trouble. "After those poor frost fae were sent to the human realm, the king sent out his troops to watch out for the remaining villages in the kingdom. Over two hundred shadow fae soldiers were lurking here. Whenever someone committed a crime, even the smallest of things, or some argument or fight broke out, the soldiers arrested everyone involved and took them away." She gulped. "Where they were taken, nobody knows. But slowly, the population of each village dropped drastically. Now, there's only a handful of fae living here. It has been hard, but we don't dare moving out."

"You're afraid of aggravating the king," Farrah muttered, her eyes hard, her arms tense. She was upset about this new information.

The fae nodded. "The soldiers moved on after there were so few of us, but I know the king still watch out for us. He's just waiting for an opportunity to take us all and erase the frost fae."

Farrah clenched her fists. "That's absurd."

"I think so too, but you better go." The fae waved us off. "If you stay here, they will soon know someone returned and they will come to check it out. Please, we don't want any trouble for our village."

Farrah's blue eyes shone with unshed tears. I could see in her demeanor, in the strain in her body, that she wanted to ask more questions, that she wanted to argue, maybe even to convince this female fae of leaving herself, but she couldn't do anything right now. She couldn't expose herself, or things would be even worse.

Farrah opened her hands and wiggled her fingers, trying to relax. "We're leaving. Please, be careful."

The fae nodded and waved us off again.

Her shoulders sagged, Farrah dragged her feet out of the village and to the cover of the trees once again. Ariella and I followed her but didn't say anything. Right now, Farrah needed time to process what she had just seen.

I just hoped she didn't close herself from me again.

15

FARRAH

WHEN WE FINALLY GOT TO MY VILLAGE, ALMOST ONE HOUR after leaving the previous one, an immense sense of pain and longing hit me. My village looked worse than I had pictured it in my head. Snow covered almost everything, including some porches and the rooftops of the houses lining the main street.

Knowing no one would come here so soon, I used my powers to open up a narrow path in the snow so Wyatt, Ariella, and I could walk to my house.

"That's your house?" Ariella asked once it came into view.

"Yes." I stared at the place where I had been raised. It was both familiar and completely strange to be back here.

Because my father had been a known general in the frost fae army, and then Daleigh too, my family's house was the largest in the village—a small manor made of wood, stone, and ice.

I walked up to the double front doors and pushed them open. A foyer greeted us, looking intact despite the many years since anyone lived here. Wrap-around ice stairs led to the second floor, and a huge crystal chandelier hung from the high ceiling. My feet echoed in the stone floor as I stepped inside.

My father and mother had walked these floors, Daleigh and I had run up and down these stairs … so many times.

"Are you okay?" Wyatt asked, his voice low.

I turned to him with a small smile. He was still standing near the doors. "Yeah, I am."

Ariella walked up to me. "All right, since you're home and you're okay, I think my mission of taking you to safety is done."

I frowned. "What do you mean?"

"I mean, I want to return to the human world," she said. "Now that you rescued me from my own grief, I want to hunt down the demons who took my wings and get my revenge."

"But …" It would be dangerous for her to face them alone. Though, I understood her. If I was in her shoes, I would have wanted the same. Besides, we had just met her, she had no reason to stay. "I understand." I picked up the medallion from my pocket. "Thank you for your help, Ariella."

She smiled at me. "Sorry we started with the wrong foot."

I shrugged. "It's all good now. I wish you good luck."

"To you too."

I sent my magic to the medallion and a portal opened up right in the middle of the foyer. Ariella waved at Wyatt and me before stepping through.

The portal closed and suddenly the house was too quiet again.

Wyatt stared at the floor.

"What is it?" I asked.

He let out a long sigh and fixed his hazel eyes on me. "Are you going to make me leave too?"

My brows curled down. "I ..." I didn't want to lie to him. Yes, I thought about getting here, making sure his wound was healed, and then sending him away. It would be safer for him if he stayed away from me. "It would be the best for you."

He took a large step toward me, cutting most of the distance between us, and I felt the heat of his strong body too close to mine. "Please, don't. I want to stay with you, Farrah."

I took a step back, needing some space from him. "Wyatt ..."

"Don't you get it?" He matched my step, putting himself right in front of me again. "I was alone and lost. I did many things I regret and make me hate myself. I had no purpose in life, no reason to keep going, nothing to fight for." He reached up and took my hand in his. "Until you came into my life. Since we first met years ago, I've been smitten by you."

Without warning, Wyatt clasped his free hand around

the nape of my neck and pulled me to him. I gasped as he leaned down and pressed his lips over mine.

For a moment, I was frozen. Then I moved my mouth with his, falling into his arms, into his sweetness, into his touch, into *him*.

This. Holy shit, this. This kiss, this moment, *this*! I had been waiting and daydreaming about this for so long. But no dream could have prepared me for how kissing Wyatt felt, for how his strong body pressed against mine made me feel, for how his big hands held on to me, heating up my skin, scorching my insides. I held on to him, as if my next breath depended on it.

But …

No, this wasn't right.

I pushed on his chest and broke the kiss. Breathing hard, I took several steps back, putting as much distance from him as I could. "This can't happen," I whispered.

Wyatt clenched his fists. "Why not? And don't you dare tell me you don't feel the same for me, because I know you do. You just showed it to me."

Damn it. It was time to tell him the truth. "Wyatt, I can't fall in love with you."

He shifted his weight, and I noticed his anger was rising. I knew it wasn't directed at me, per se, but it still made me wary. "Why? Because I'm not a fae? Because I'm a lone wolf? Because I've been lost? Why, tell me why?"

"Because!" I shouted, getting irritated myself. "Because there's a damn curse!" I let a long breath out to steady myself. I continued, my voice back to normal, "After

Daleigh brought the human he loved here and the fae king killed her and banished us, he cast a cursed on all the fae in and out of the fae realm to prevent us from loving anyone outside of our own race. If I was to love you, I would lose my immortality and my magic. I'll be forced to live life as a human. And eventually, I'll die."

Maybe he didn't care about that, because as a werewolf, he would someday die anyway. He would live a lot longer than humans, but he would still grow old and die.

Wyatt's hands relaxed and his shoulders sagged. The anger left his face, replaced by concern. "There must be a way of breaking the spell."

I shook my head. "There's not."

Wyatt paced on the other side of the foyer. I waited patiently, not willing to say anything else about this matter. I was sure of my feelings for him, but was it worth it to love him and then die? I would eventually leave him alone when I died, and he would mourn me. I didn't want that for him.

Suddenly, Wyatt halted and faced me again. "All right. I will leave this place, but I'll stay close by, in the fae realm, from where I can protect you in case anything goes wrong."

That wasn't the best plan. "Wyatt—"

"You won't see me, and I won't see you," he continued, interrupting me. "I won't bother you unless you need my help." He pressed his lips tight. "Please, Farrah, let me do at least that."

I stared at him, the gleam in his eyes breaking my

heart. I didn't want him to go, but I couldn't have him here either. The temptation to surrender to him was too great and I wasn't strong enough to resist it. Not for long.

But ... we had just arrived, and his wound was still healing. He needed some rest before I sent him away. I inhaled sharply, knowing I would regret my decision. "You can stay, but not here." I gestured to the door. "You can take one of the empty houses in the village, as long as you stay hidden."

The corner of his lips started to move up, but he forced himself to stay serious. "That works."

I grabbed the healing salve I had stolen earlier and gave it to him. "Apply this three times a day. When you're fully healed, let me know. We can talk about the next step then." The next step being opening a portal so he could leave, but I didn't want to say that out loud.

Wyatt took a step back. "Thanks."

Then he was gone. Out the door and into the snow again.

I stared at the white view outside, my heart clenching. What had I just done?

I PICKED A SMALL HOUSE NOT TOO CLOSE TO FARRAH'S family manor, but from where I could see it if I stepped out on the porch. For a couple of days, I just cleaned up the house, hunted for food in the forest, applied the healing salve on my wound, and rested.

From the little I could see, Farrah was also cleaning up her family's place, and looking in the other houses, searching for useful things left behind. Like me, she hunted for food using her powers, and she also ventured into a nearby village twice to buy more food and other things.

Meanwhile, I put my mind to work.

I wouldn't go down without a fight. I needed a chance, just one small chance, to make things right and stay beside Farrah. And that meant finding a way to take down the fae king.

After making sure Farrah was safe, I shapeshifted into

my wolf form, left my new house, and ventured into the shadow court. The dark forest, the tall trees, the gray skies ... this place was too fucking creepy, but I didn't stop. It wasn't too hard to stay hidden in the darkness of the forest as I advanced toward the castle.

It was hard to miss it—the dark palace made of shiny stone jutting out from the rough ground and piercing the sky. I slowed down and stayed behind some trees as I observed the happenings around the castle.

As expected, it was heavily guarded by soldiers dressed in black, though I noticed a few fae dressed in simple vests and dresses entering the castle through a back entrance —servants.

If only I could glamour myself ...

I couldn't do that, but I could do the next best thing: I shifted back into my human form, went to the nearest village where I stole fae clothing, makeup, and even a bottle of perfume. Then I dressed up, ruffled my hair so it covered the tips of my ears, applied some makeup to make as pale as the fae, and sprayed a ton of perfume all over myself, trying to disguise my werewolf scent.

Then I steeled myself and joined the fae walking toward the castle's back entrance. I received a few side glances. Maybe they were wondering if I was new, or they didn't like the scent of my perfume, but hopefully, they couldn't tell I wasn't one of them.

To my surprise, I didn't have any trouble getting into the palace. The problem was moving inside without being seen when so many fucking soldiers patrolled every hallway I came across. In less than ten minutes here, I had already seen at least thirty different soldiers. And that was only inside the palace. How many more were on the outside?

Armed with a broom and a bucket, I stopped and pretended to clean the floors each time I heard footsteps coming closer to where I was. I didn't think too much about what I was doing, because if I did, I would question the logic of my plan. I didn't have time for logic.

After getting lost trying to find the main hall and where the king could possibly be, I finally found him in the throne room with two other male fae whose armor was more elaborate than the others. They were probably generals or something.

Hidden behind a tall, thick stone column, I spied out and took a look at the infamous shadow king. He was tall, probably half a head taller than me, and even though his shoulders were narrow, he irradiated power and strength. With the elegant black clothing and a black crown atop his long, black hair, the fae king didn't ask for attention. He demanded it.

I gulped down, momentarily taken back.

If this guy was as powerful as he looked, I didn't stand a chance against him, unless I took him by surprise.

With him standing in the center of the throne room with two capable soldiers, I couldn't attack now, or I was fucking dead meat.

So I waited. People came and went, bringing things to

the fae king, reporting on things, and soldiers coming to check in on things.

My legs were cramping when finally, a couple of hours later, the king informed his soldiers that he would be going to his chambers. I frowned as he walked out of the throne room, followed by no less than six soldiers. Did he usually stay alone in his chambers?

With no time to waste, I exited the throne room and followed a servant until I found the narrow hallways that cut through the castle, allowing the servants to move around unseen.

"Excuse me," I asked an old female fae who could barely hold on to the tray in her hands. "I'm new here. Where's the fae king's chambers? I have something I need to bring to him."

"Follow those stairs." She pointed to an opening behind her. "Go to the last floor."

"Thank you," I muttered as I rushed by her. I had to get there before the king.

I took three steps at a time, went up four floors, and arrived at a narrow black door. I opened just a crack and looked inside. The huge, dark chambers seemed to be still empty.

I quickly snuck in, hid inside a closet, and shifted into a werewolf. I tried not paying attention to anything around me, just in slowing my breathing and being quiet.

It didn't take long for the king to walk in his chambers, followed by some guards and a servant. After a few orders, he shooed them all out.

I spied out of the door. The king was standing in the middle of his chambers, his back to me, his hands on his waist, his head hung low.

This was my chance.

My heart racing, I tiptoed out of the closet and pounced on the king's back, aiming for his neck.

In a flash, the king twisted around, his dark eyes shining. He extended his hand toward me and shadows enveloped around me, pushing me back.

"Oh my, oh my." The king clamped his hands on his back and stared at me, amused. "You think I haven't sensed your presence? Since you first stepped into the throne room, I knew you're a werewolf."

I jerked against the shadows, trying to break free, but couldn't. They were too strong for me.

The fae king tilted his head. "Won't you shift back and talk to me? How insolent." He tsked, as if disappointed in me. Was the motherfucker having fun with this? "Guards!"

Shadow fae soldiers burst into the chambers. When their eyes landed on me, they pointed their spears at me. "Take this werewolf to the dungeons. I'll *play* with it later."

Play sounded more like torture.

No, I wouldn't stay here for this.

The shadow magic retreated and I acted.

I jumped on the fae king, but he flicked his hand, sending me flying to the other side of the chambers. I yelped as a side table broke my fall, hurting my side. On top of the table was a small mirror-like object. It seemed important. So I closed my mouth around it and ran.

"Get him!" the fae king shouted, causing the wall of the castle to shake.

But I didn't stop, my only thought on the rapid steps of my paws. I weaved through the guards, and other soldiers who flocked the hallways. I felt magic rippling behind me as the king and his soldiers tried to catch me. It wouldn't take long for it.

So I jumped off the nearest balcony. My limbs jarred from the impact of the hard ground, but I didn't stop. I broke off into a run, fleeing the castle.

17

FARRAH

It took me a long time to clean up my old chambers and the kitchen—at least two rooms I needed if I was going to stay here for a while. Though the kitchen's pantry needed to be stocked, I was surprised to see all my old clothes still hanging in my closet. They were a little dusty and some smelled like they were rotting, but I was able to salvage a handful of dresses and a thick cloak that would serve me until I got something better.

After a couple of days just working on the manor and hunting for food in the back forest, I decided it was time to go to the nearest market to buy some more food and other things I would need.

As I downed my cloak and stepped out of the manor, I glanced around to the many abandoned houses, wondering which one Wyatt had chosen. Knowing him, I was sure he wouldn't have picked the closest one, but he wouldn't have been too far in case I needed help.

As I walked by the main street, I looked at each house, but I couldn't tell which one he was living in —temporarily.

I let out a long sigh. Damn, I couldn't let him stay for long. Soon, I should check on him, see how his wound was healing, and to talk to him about leaving. The longer he stayed here, the worst it would be later.

That had been our deal, hadn't it? He would help me get away, then he would leave. We did that. I was away, even if not exactly where we had first planned to go, but I was safe now, and hopefully, I would be even safer when I went to Europe.

When would I go to Europe, though?

I wondered about that as I walked to the nearest village that wasn't abandoned—one across the border of Woods Court. No one knew I was here now. I could hide here for a while ... for a long while. Then, when I felt it wasn't working anymore, I moved on. There was nothing for me in Europe anyway. My life had become just this: hiding wherever I could. Did it really make a difference if I hid here or in another realm?

Besides, I had missed this place. It felt so good to be back here. I could feel the snow and ice and cold in my veins, in my lungs, in my heart. This was where I belonged ...

And because of that, I couldn't stay for long. I knew that.

Finally, I arrived at the village in the Woods Court. After glamouring my hair so it would look a dark brown and my eyes so they would be green, I went to the market. A smile stretched over my lips as I walked down the stone paved street with several stands flanked it, selling everything from spices and warm cakes, to clothing and jewelry, and much more. The scents of vanilla and cinnamon and other spices filled the air, making my mouth water.

With a wicker basket in my arms, I stopped by a stand selling spices and produce and hovered my hands over the bowls full of goodies, thinking about what I could cook with those. It had been a while since I cooked fae food and I missed it.

"I'm serious," a female said in a hushed tone. She stood on the other side of the tent, talking to a male fae. "The rumor is going all around."

The male shook his head. "I heard many rumors before, but this one takes the title. A werewolf trying to kill the fae king? That's ridiculous."

The blood rushed out of my veins and my heart slowed to a crawl.

"Excuse me?" I asked, leaning over the stand. "You're saying a werewolf entered the palace."

The female glanced side to side before approaching me. "Yes, that's what I heard. Though, a werewolf in the fae realm? That does seem like stretching it."

I frowned, knowing very well that it could happen. "Does the rumor say anything? Like, what happened to the werewolf?" I held my breath, afraid of her answer.

"He got away," she said. "The king sent hordes of soldiers after him. If the rumors are true, soon we should hear about the soldiers catching a werewolf." She shook her head, her lips pressed tight. "I bet the fae king will have a public execution for him, another example of what he does to his enemies and anyone who defies him."

My stomach dropped. A horde of soldiers after him? A public execution?

Without another word, I whirled around and walked away. Away from the village, away from my house. I dropped the basket and set out on a run, as fast as I could, in the direction of the Shadow court.

What the hell was Wyatt thinking? Attacking the fae king? Hadn't I told him the damn king was too powerful? Why hadn't he listened to me?

I must have run for hours, scouring the forest, hoping that I would cross paths with Wyatt. I prayed for all the gods and nature and forces of the fae and human realm, just to be lucky enough to find him.

And then, I did.

Across from a valley, a werewolf ran as fast as a bullet. A massive group of shadow fae chased him, yelling obscenities and occasionally throwing magic at him, and missing only by a hairsbreadth.

Soon, they would catch up with Wyatt ... and kill him.

I THOUGHT THAT ONCE I WAS OUT OF THE CASTLE, IT WOULD be easy to outrun the fae and hide, but I underestimated them.

I underestimated the fae king.

What the fuck had I done? Just because I had helped Luana and Keeran defeat evil warlords before, because I had fought demons beside Rey, I believed I could take on a powerful fae by myself?

That had been stupid, but in my defense, I wasn't thinking. I was just feeling. My love for Farrah was too great, too strong. I couldn't imagine a life without her. I had to find a way to break the curse that didn't allow her to love anyone else, and right now the only way I saw was to kill the fucking king.

Big, stupid move.

The looking glass in between my jaws rattled my teeth with each ripple of my muscles.

My paws hit the ground hard and fast as I ran from the many shadow fae soldiers on my tail. The looking glass in between my jaws rattled my teeth with each ripple of my muscles. I had no idea where I was going, I just knew I couldn't stop running or they would kill me.

Though, after almost two hours chasing me, the fae was finally getting closer. I could hear their heavy footsteps behind me, their shouts to run faster, to throw magic at me.

And that was what they did. With bows made of shadow, they sent shadow arrows at me. I started zigzagging on the forest, trying to avoid the hits. Some landed scarily close to my paws.

I gulped and pushed myself harder.

Werewolves were fast, but I didn't think I had ever run this fast. The adrenaline and fear filled my veins, and if it wasn't for them, I was sure I would have collapsed long ago.

I arrived at a large valley of lush green grass and colorful flowers. Behind it, I could see the snowcapped mountains in the distance. Should I go into the Frost Court? What if they followed me there and soon found Farrah too?

I didn't have time to mull over it as an arrow grazed my hind leg. I snarled but kept going, across the valley.

I went down the valley, and that was when everything went wrong. The fae didn't run behind me. They flew. They flew down the valley in graceful jumps, landing very, very close to me.

Then they shot their arrows.

One pierced one of my hind legs, another got into my back, and many more grazed my fur and skin, making it hard for me to keep going.

The adrenaline faded away, my vision blurred, my movements slowed.

I was done for.

Until someone ran to me.

All I saw was white. A silhouette in white rushed to me, her hands lifted high. A blast of cold hit me, easing the searing heat spreading through my body. My savior rushed into me, holding me in her arms.

Then the white faded, and I fell into the darkness.

A STAB OF PAIN COURSED THROUGH MY BODY AND I JERKED awake, suddenly panicked. The last thing I remembered was fleeing from the shadow fae soldiers.

"Easy there," a voice I knew very well said. Farrah sat down beside me in a narrow bed and pressed her hand on my bare chest, pushing me back down on the mattress.

"What happened?" I asked, my voice hoarse, realizing I was naked with a blanket over my legs and hips, leaving my chest exposed.

Farrah let out a long sigh. "You were stupid enough to try taking out the fae king?" Her delicate brows curled down. "What the hell were you thinking? You could have gotten yourself killed!"

"Apparently, I wasn't thinking." I tried turning to the side, but pain laced my movements.

"You can say that again." She shook her head. "I found you and froze the soldiers in place. It didn't last long, but it was enough for us to get away." Her shoulders drooped. "But by now the fae king knows I'm here and that I helped a werewolf escape."

I glanced around, worried. The walls around us were made of wood, not ice. "We aren't at your family's manor, are we?"

Farrah shook her head. "No. I'm sure the shadow fae are already there, searching for us." She turned a hand, as if introducing me to the house. "This is a cottage at the edge of the Blaze Court. It belonged to my great-grandmother. I don't think the fae king knows about it."

Fuck. I had made everything worse. As usual, I hadn't thought of the consequences if I failed. And I had failed big this time. Now, not only the fae king was still alive, but he was on the hunt for me *and* Farrah. This place, which should have been her hideout for a while, was now compromised, and it was all my fault.

"I'm sorry," I muttered, suddenly ashamed of my actions.

Farrah exhaled through her nose. "Just ... lay down and be a good patient." She touched the side of my stomach, where a damp piece of cloth was against my skin. "I was able to take the two arrows out and stop the bleeding. I applied some healing salve on the wounds and the scratches on your legs and arms. If you rest, you'll be fine in a couple of days."

She started rising from the bed, but I reached out and held on to her wrist. "Thank you," I said, my voice heavy with emotion. "For coming for me."

Her brilliant blue eyes met mine, a sad shine in them. It cut my heart in half. She didn't say anything. She just stared at me for a few seconds, then gently pulled her arm from my grasp and walked away.

Farrah was disappointed in me, as she should be.

FARRAH

WYATT SLEPT ON AND OFF FOR THREE DAYS WHILE HIS wounds healed. To sped up things, I had glamoured myself and ventured into a village where I acquired some strong healing herbs and other things we would need. I changed the dressing of his wounds at least twice a day, making sure the healing salve was acting as it should.

Thankfully, fae herbs had special properties and when mixed in the right way, they could do almost anything.

Healing two arrow wounds plus several scratches in a handful of days was one of these amazing things.

On the fourth day, Wyatt finally rose from the bed and came into the kitchen to eat with me. His steps were slow and every once in a while, he winced, as if his wounds still hurt. I hoped they did. He deserved to hurt for a little while longer for what he did.

"Sit," I said, gesturing to the table on the corner of the kitchen. Groaning, he took one of the chairs, and I brought the creamy soup I had made to the table. "Eat. It's full of herbs that will help you heal."

In silence, Wyatt picked up the ladle and the bowl and served himself.

We ate in tense silence, my mind whirling with so many thoughts. Even after a few days, I was still sad and disappointed with him, and angry too. I pressed my mouth, keeping all the words I wanted to shout inside.

Halfway through the meal, Wyatt dropped his spoon. "Talk to me." The sorrowful tone of his voice tugged at my heart. This wasn't fair.

"I really don't want to talk," I said, my voice tight.

"I know you want to yell at me. Then yell at me. I deserve it."

Shaking my head, I lifted my eyes to his. "At least, you know it." Not hungry anymore, I rose from the chair, picked up my bowl, and walked to the kitchen counter.

"Farrah ..." Wyatt started. I dropped the bowl on the sink and leaned on the counter. "Talk to me, please."

I whirled around and glared at him. "Talk to you? Yell at you? That isn't enough. I know you know the mess you just caused. How could you be this stupid?" I had already asked him this when he first woke up after I rescued him, but I couldn't help it.

Wyatt rose from his seat. "I just wanted to help you!"

"Help me? You made things worse now!"

"That wasn't my intention."

I crossed my arms. "Then what was your intention?

Because certainly, you didn't really believe you could take the fae king on your own."

"I thought ..." He ran a hand over his shaggy hair. It was getting longer and unruly. "I thought that if I took him by surprise, I would be able to kill him." He took a few steps toward me. "I thought that if I killed him, then the curse would be lifted and you would open your heart to me."

My breath caught. He had done it for me? Of course he had. "Wyatt ..." I started, my tone lower, though I wasn't sure what to say to him.

His handsome face closed up in a scowl. "Don't bother. I'm tired of you being mad at me." He shuffled his feet toward the door. "I'll leave."

At that, I rushed toward him and grabbed his arm. "No, you won't. As much as I want to put some distance between us, you just proved to me you can't be left alone. Besides, you're hurt and shadow fae are scouring the fae realm after us. We need to stay put."

He pulled his arm from my grip, his expression still hard. "I just ... I need some fresh air. I'll go for a quick walk around the cottage."

I opened my mouth to argue with him but closed it again. I had to remember he was a werewolf and he needed to go for a run sometimes. Even if it was still too painful for him to change into his wolf because of his injures, he could at least enjoy the warmer weather of the border and clear his head.

I watched as he stomped out of the cottage, my heart

clenching for all the things going wrong between us.

***

I PACED AROUND THE SMALL FAMILY ROOM IN THE COTTAGE, wondering where Wyatt had gone. He had been gone for almost two hours and that worried me. How much more should I wait until it was acceptable for me to go after him?

After another thirty minutes, I caved. I turned to the door ... and it opened before I could touch it. Wyatt walked in.

"Hey," he muttered, looking at me.

"Um, where have you been?" I asked, controlling my tone. I wasn't mad. I was worried.

"I remembered I stole something from the fae king." He lifted his hand, something clutched in between his fingers. "I had it in between my teeth while I was in wolf form, but I dropped it once I started losing consciousness."

I frowned. "So you went back to retrieve it?" We were very far away from where I had found him. He had gone deep into the forest, where the shadow fae could have found him and attacked him. A new wave of anger built up inside me.

"It looked important." He opened his hand.

A gasp escaped my throat and my anger flew out the window. "That's ... that's a looking glass." I stared at the small, round see-through glass with an adorned silver frame. "No wonder the king is after you so bad. It's probably the only one of its kind."

Wyatt handed it to me. "What does it do?"

I gingerly picked it up and held it as if it could break at any second. "Supposedly, it shows what is, what will be, and what might be."

Wyatt furrowed. "You mean, about anything?"

"I think so."

"Let's use it."

I held tightly to the looking glass. "I'm not sure that's a good idea. I've heard of legends of fae who went crazy after seeing whatever it showed them. They couldn't handle it." I glanced at the object in my hands. "Sometimes it's better not to know your future."

"Farrah, what are you afraid of?" Wyatt asked, sounding skeptical. "If this shows the future, it'll let us know if the fae prince will win, or if you'll be able to get away from him forever."

"Remember, it also shows what *might* be. Even if it shows that I get away from him, that might change."

Wyatt puffed his chest out. "I want to know."

The truth was, I also wanted to know. I was just afraid of what the looking glass might show.

I inhaled deeply, willing courage to fill me. "All right." I clutched the looking glass, closed my eyes, and thought about its magic. "Here we go."

I opened my eyes and glanced down at it. The glass turned opaque as colorful shadows swirled within it, like figures taking place in a mirror.

It was working.

At first, nothing happened. Colorful smoke swirled inside the looking glass, and I wondered if the fucking thing was broken or if Farrah didn't know how to use it.

But then the smoke faded away, revealing a scene, like watching a TV screen. I leaned over Farrah's shoulder to take a better look.

In the scene, Daleigh entered a big, white tent, where dozens of cots were spread, and dozens of fae lay on them. With a grim expression, Daleigh knelt beside an old male.

Beside me, Farrah inhaled a sharp breath.

That was when I realized the male wasn't old. His magic had left him and he was slowly dying. Holding his hand tight, Daleigh whispered something to him. In a moment, the male fae closed his eyes and his hand went slack.

Daleigh gritted his teeth. But when he looked out to

the rest of the fae in the cots, his face wasn't angry. It was painful, hopeless, desperate.

Smoke flooded the glass's surface and I thought it was done, but another scene appeared.

This time, I took in a sudden breath, my heart clenching.

Farrah was wearing a beautiful white dress and she stood beside Prince Lark, her hand in his. She smiled at him as he raised their hands and announced their marriage. The hundreds of fae gathered at the throne room knelt before them and lowered their heads.

"What the fuck," I muttered.

But the looking glass wasn't done.

The scene changed on more time, showing Farrah and I kissing in a strange bed, our clothes on the floor. My heart sped up and my chest tightened with hope and desire.

Then the scene was gone along with the smoke and the looking glass returned to its original state.

Beside me, Farrah stared at it, her face paler than usual.

"Farrah," I whispered. "Are you okay?"

She shook her head before turning bright, desperate eyes to me. "No, I'm not." She pushed the glass toward me. "I have to go." She started marching away, but I held on to her wrist.

"What are you doing? Where are you going?"

She didn't fight against my grip. "I can't let that happen, Wyatt. The fae are losing their magic and dying. The longer they stay away from the fae realm, the worst it'll be. More and more of them will die. And it's all because of me. Because I'm being selfish."

"You're not selfish."

"Yes, I am. What's the life of one fae when it could save hundreds? Thousands?" She shook her head. "I can't do this anymore. I can't ignore it. I have to go back to the human realm. I have to go to Prince Lark." She pulled her hand from my grip, but I didn't let her go.

"We can change what the glass showed us," I said, my voice coarse with emotion. She could *not* marry that fucking prince. "We can find a way to make it all—"

"Wyatt!" She finally broke free of my grasp, her fearful, beautiful face now fierce, her eyes sparkling with anger. "I'm tired of running, of hiding, and this proves it's for nothing." She gestured toward the looking glass in my hand.

"You told me the looking glass shows what *might* be. So you marrying the prince is still out in the open."

Farrah shook her head. "No, Wyatt. The glass shows what is, what will be, and what might be. In that order." She held her head high. "You and I will probably never happen. It's better not to hope for it."

My chest seized as I glanced down at the looking glass. So ... the glass had just teased about Farrah and me? About the future I had been waiting, just to take it away from me? Was this some kind of fucking joke?

I shook my head. "No, I refuse to believe that."

"Believe what you want," she said, turning her back to

me. She fished the medallion from her pocket and started casting the spell to open the portal. Agony hit me hard in the chest. She was going to the human world to give herself to the evil fae prince.

Before she could, I took two steps to her and held her arm again, stopping her from finishing the spell. "Please, don't do this."

She turned her blue eyes to me, shining with unshed tears. "I have to." Her voice broke. "If I don't, my people will die."

I loomed over her. "We'll find a way to save them, I promise. Just ... don't throw away what we have. You and I belong together, you know that. We've belonged together since the first time we met. Admit it."

Despair gleamed across her eyes. "Wyatt, please don't make this more difficult than it already is."

"This, what? Us? Our feelings for each other? Our entwined fate?" Slowly, I reached over and rested my hand on her cheek, running my thumb on her smooth skin. "We can't run from each other any more than the fucking moon can't help but rising after the sun has gone down."

I didn't let her protest. I lowered my mouth to hers and kissed her. This time, she didn't hesitate. Her lips met with mine stroke by stroke, our tongues entwining in a delicious dance.

When close to her, desire always ran underneath my skin. Sometimes, I had to push it down, to reign it in, before I lost it. Now, I wanted to lose it. I let my desire free and ran my hands around her shoulders, down her back, pressing her against me.

With a sigh, Farrah melted into me.

It was all the signal I needed. I scooped her up in my arms and took her to the bedroom. Without breaking the kiss, I set her down on her feet, and worked on getting rid of our clothes. As desperate as me, Farrah helped me, almost ripping my shirt off its seams.

Once she was completely naked, I took a second to pull back and admire her beauty. Holy fuck, she was everything. She was my entire soul, heart, and mind. And I knew I was hers. She couldn't deny it, not when she looked me with those two sapphires turned molten by her own desire.

I gently pushed her back and laid her down in the bed. Staring into her eyes, I covered her delicious body with mine. She moaned when I positioned myself in between her legs, but she didn't break my stare. The anticipation alone would kill me. Slowly, I slipped inside her. And then I felt it.

The immense sensation, the desperate feeling, the tight rope around my heart.

The mating bond.

Farrah was my mate.

She gasped, as if she too had felt that.

I lost it. I covered her mouth with mine and kissed her hard and deep, while I thrust into her, even harder and deeper.

Together, we drowned in lust and love, in pure ecstasy.

And I wondered if I would ever be able to recover from this.

<hr>

THE BED WAS SOFT UNDER ME, THE WOOL BLANKET HEAVY over my body. The memory from last night inundated my mind even before I opened my eyes and a smile stretched over my lips.

I had done it. I had convinced Farrah to stay with me, and we had made love. The mating bond has snapped. I was sure she had felt it too. Now we really belonged to each other, just as it was supposed to be.

Opening my eyes, I turned to my side, ready to pull her to me, even if she was still sleeping.

My eyes went wide and my heart squeezed in my chest.

The other side of the bed was empty. I glanced around the bedroom, barely taking the place in. I hadn't been here before, and last night it was dark and I was busy. I couldn't have cared less about the bedroom when she had been in my arms.

I opened my mouth to call her ... maybe she was in the bathroom? Or downstairs in the kitchen. But I wasn't stupid. I knew what happened.

A dull pain started around my heart.

Farrah had gone to the human realm to marry the fae prince.

21

FARRAH

Leaving Wyatt behind in my bedroom, in my bed, had been one of the most difficult things I had done in my life.

His words echoed in my mind. *You and I belong together, you know that.*

It was true, and last night only served to prove it. When I felt the mating bond snapping, I almost told him. But there was no need. I was sure he had felt it too. Deep down, I always knew Wyatt was my mate. This just proved it.

But I was done being selfish. I had been selfish for three years. I had only thought about my safety and what I wanted. I couldn't do that anymore. Daleigh was right. I had no right to abandon my people to save my own skin. We had been sent to this realm together, we had been banished and punished together, we had survived together.

And now I would end their misery. Even if that meant starting mine.

When I made my decision before sunrise this morning, I opened the portal a couple of miles from Prince Lark's Shade Fortress. I could have created a portal directly by the front door, but I needed time to clear my mind and come to terms with what I was about to do.

So I walked with heavy feet toward his castle, my mind churning, each step making it harder for me to keep moving.

But I had to. I had already decided. I would do it, no matter what.

It took me a while, but finally, I felt my mind clearing, my core becoming numb ... that was the only way I would survive this.

Then, in the distance, the Shade Fortress appeared in front of a green mountain, shining dark under the midday sun. A tall structure with many towers, round balconies, and dark vines swirling over the stone walls.

My new home.

I paused, trying to come to terms with it. Damn it, I thought I was done thinking about this by now.

"Don't do it," a voice came from my left.

I spun around, calling my magic and letting it fill my veins. I blinked, staring at Ariella. "What are you doing here?"

Approaching me, the fallen angel shrugged. "After I came back to the human realm, something kept nagging at me. I knew it was just time before you did something stupid. So I decided to come this way. I was hoping my gut was wrong, but it rarely is."

I frowned. "What, you came to say goodbye?"

"No, I came to stop you," she said, her eyes locked on mine.

I shook my head. "What do you care?"

She lowered her gaze for a brief moment. "Because I've seen this before. I've seen pure souls sacrificing themselves for others. It never works the way they hoped it would work. In fact, it only made everything worse." She took a careful step closer, her hand over her stomach. "I don't know what it is, but I can feel it right here. Whatever you're planning, it won't work."

"I'm not planning anything," I said, my voice even. "I won't fight anymore. I'll surrender to Prince Lark and he'll let my people go back home. It's that simple."

"I don't think it'll be simple."

I took in a long breath, growing annoyed with this exchange. "I won't be stopped, Ariella. If you try, I'm gonna fight you."

"Then we're going to fight."

Ariella threw her arms out, but I was ready. Her light hit the ice wall I conjured, breaking it in a million pieces. She had proven to be strong, but I was strong too.

Besides, if I wasted time with a battle, my resolution might falter.

I couldn't afford that.

Gritting my teeth, I sent all my power to her. A dozen ice soldiers appeared before her, separating us.

"Goodbye, Ariella," I whispered.

I didn't stay to see her easily defeating my ice soldiers. All I needed was to buy myself some time. Without another look back, I darted toward the Shade Fortress.

"Farrah, no!" she screamed.

I ignored her and kept running.

When the fortress loomed over me, I allowed myself to slow down. The shadow fae soldiers guarding the front gates saw me coming and pointed their spears at me.

But then they recognized me and lowered their weapons.

"Take me to Prince Lark," I told them, my chin high, my chest puffed. I might be doing this against my will, but I wouldn't look put down by it. My pride would be intact.

I hoped.

The guards hastily opened the gates. They guided me inside the fortress, through a large foyer and long corridors, until the double doors of the grand hall stood before me.

The guards pushed the doors open.

And I marched inside.

22

WYATT

DESPITE KNOWING WHERE FARRAH HAD GONE, I LOOKED FOR her around the small cottage like a fucking fool. I had to be wrong. I had to be. After last night, she couldn't just up and leave me ... and go marry some other guy.

The anger swelled in me, my werewolf temper rising fast. When I finally stopped at the cottage's entrance, I punched the door with all my strength. The door ripped from its hinging and landed several feet away in the snow.

All right, letting my anger take over wasn't helping. I inhaled deeply and ran a hand over my hair, trying to think. I needed a fucking medallion to go back to the human world and stop her.

But how would I get one?

I quickly put on my shoes and a thick cloak, and marched away from the cottage. If I was supposed to find a medallion, it wouldn't be here.

With the hood of my cloak covering my hair and ears, I

went to the two nearest villages and searched for officials, or high ranked fae, or a soldier … anyone who could have a medallion on them.

But besides receiving some suspicious glances, I found nothing. So I went on to the next village, while thinking that I might have to purposely run into the shadow fae soldiers who were looking for me. I bet one of them had the medallion. I could snatch it and use it before they actually held me down and killed me.

"Come on down, Rusty," a voice said.

I glanced around the forest, but only saw trees and bushes. The sun was high now in the Wood Court, and the scent of pine and moss filled the air.

"Rusty, don't be stubborn," the voice said again.

I halted and strained my hearing, trying to pinpoint where the voice was coming from. The person asked Rusty to come again, and I followed the voice, until I was standing before an old fae.

The male fae turned to me with kind, gray eyes. He was short for fae standards and with too many wrinkles. "Can you help me?" He pointed up the tree. "My cat is stuck and doesn't want to come down."

I glanced up the tree. An orange cat with pointed furry ears, sharp teeth, and claws, held on to a tall, thin branch.

I frowned. Wasn't this male a fae? Wasn't the cat a fae? Why did they need my help? I let out an annoyed sigh. Better just help them and move on before my anger rose again.

"All right," I muttered, taking off my cloak.

Using my werewolf strength, I scaled up the tree. When I reached the branch, the cat didn't want to come with me. It even snarled at me, which spiked my temper. This motherfucker ...

I grabbed the cat, ignoring the way it jerked in my grasp, and jumped down. The moment I handed the cat to the old fae, it relaxed in its owner's arms and, I swear, it shot me a knowing smile.

What the fuck?

"Thank you," the old fae said. "I couldn't have done that without you."

"It was nothing." I wiped my hands on my pants, then picked up the cloak from the ground. "I should go."

"I know," the old fae said. "You're the werewolf hiding from the fae king." I stared at him, hoping he wouldn't turn me in after I just helped him. The old fae ran his hand on the top of the cat's head, down to the middle of its back. "I'm Spencer, and I think I can help you."

I frowned. He wanted to help me? "How?"

"I can open a portal so you can go back to the human realm. Isn't that what you want?"

I blinked. "You have a medallion?"

Spencer nodded. "I do. And I also have this." He fished a small blue pendant and thin chain from his pocket. "You should give this to the one you're after. She'll need it."

"How ... how do you know?"

Spencer shrugged. "I just know." He pushed the pendant in my hands.

I took it, staring at the simple blue stone. "What does it do?"

"Ah, you'll have to wait and see," Spencer said, sounding enigmatic.

Who cared what it did? As long as he opened the portal for me, he could give me mud in a bowl and tell me it was soup and I would fucking eat it. If for some reason later I found out the pendant was dangerous, I would get rid of it.

"I'll give this to her," I said, tucking the pendant into one of my pockets.

Spencer pulled the medallion from under his heavy shirt. "Are you ready?" I nodded, my muscles tense with anticipation. This was being easier than I thought it would be. "Good luck."

The portal appeared a couple of feet in front of me.

"Thank you," I said to the old fae.

Then I stepped into the portal.

23

FARRAH

I TOOK THREE STEPS INTO THE MAIN HALL AND STOPPED DEAD in my tracks. In the front of the black dais at the end of the room, my brother knelt on the cold floor, his head hanging low.

"Please, Prince Lark, reconsider," he asked, his tone desperate.

Seated on his black throne, Prince Lark's dark eyes rose from my brother to me. The corners of his lips turned up.

My stomach twisted in knots. Prince Lark was beautiful in a gloomy kind of way. With long black hair, thick eyebrows, and sharp angles to his face. A black crown sat on top of his head, and he downed a black suit, his thick cloak embroidered with silver details. He was beautiful, but he was also terrifying. Underneath that powerful facade, he was purely evil.

"I think we can arrange something," Prince Lark said, standing up.

My brother looked at him, confused. Then he followed Lark's gaze and found me behind him. "Farrah," he whispered, relieved.

"I'm here now," I spoke, my voice firm despite the trembling inside my chest. "You can pardon the frost fae and let them go back to our realm."

"That's wonderful news." Lark snapped his fingers. A soldier came forward with a sleek black box. He halted before my brother and handed the box to him. "A deal is a deal," Lark said. "Your medallions are in the box. You and your people are pardoned. Take the medallions to them and go back to the fae realm."

With wide eyes, Daleigh clutched to the box. He turned to me, still looking shocked to see me here. "You came," he said, approaching me.

I nodded. "Take these to our people. Take them home."

He reached for me, clasped his hand around my shoulder. "Thank you for doing this."

I nodded again, not sure how to answer him. "Just go."

A frown appeared between his brows. "Will you come to visit us?"

"Of course." Though to be honest, we all knew I would be living like a prisoner now. I would go visit only if I was allowed to.

"Take care," he whispered, his voice full of emotion.

"You too." I gently pushed his hand away. "Now go. You have no time to waste."

Daleigh's eyes held mine for a few more seconds, then he dashed away from the main hall. Once he was out of sight, I let out a long breath. At least, that was done. In a couple of hours, Daleigh and our people would be safely back in their village, where they would restart and build a new, prosperous life.

The doors closed with a loud thud. Still holding his creepy grin, Lark walked up to me. "You finally came to your senses."

"Sorry it took me so long," I lied.

"It's okay. I confess I like a good chase, especially when I know I'll eventually win." He gestured toward me. "See? You're here now, aren't you?"

I lifted my chin, trying to erase the nasty, sick tone of his voice and glint of his eyes. "So, when will be the wedding?"

"Tonight!"

My heart sank.

"But ..." My mind raced, trying to think of excuses to delay the inevitable. "The party, the invitations, the dress, and—"

Lark dismissed me with a wave of his hand. "It's all taken care of. All you need to do is follow your new hand-maiden—" he beckoned someone over. From the corner of the room, a young female fae stepped closer, his head lowered—"to your chambers where you'll get ready."

"Glad you're so thoughtful," I said, my voice strained. If Lark noticed it, he pretended he didn't.

"Now run along." He wiggled his fingers at the hand-maiden. "We've got much to do before the wedding tonight."

"This way, my lady," the young fae said in a meek tone.

I followed her out of the main hall. As she guided me through the hallways toward my chambers, I kept sneaking glances out the windows, feeling as if I had just checked into a prison.

I wished it was only a feeling, but I knew it was real now.

24

I DIDN'T CARE HOW SPENCER KNEW ABOUT FARRAH, ABOUT what was happening to her, and how he knew where to open the portal for me. But once I crossed it, I recognized the place. I hadn't been on this road for almost three years, but once I had walked this path with Farrah and Luana, when we had come to the Shade Fortress to steal the Dagger of All Hunting.

When Farrah made a terrible promise to Prince Lark.

I started shifting into my wolf form when someone called me.

"Wyatt!"

I snapped to the voice's direction and was surprised to see Ariella walking toward me. No, not walking. Limping. I frowned. "What are you doing here?"

"I tried to stop her," she said, her voice low and tired. Her blue eyes were distraught. "But she conjured ice soldiers to fight me." She halted and shifted her weight, getting off her bad leg. "That was hours ago and just now I was able to defeat the last one."

I gritted my teeth. "So ... she's inside the Shade Fortress now?"

Ariella nodded.

Fuck.

"Also ..." she started. "I saw a bunch of fae heading to the fortress earlier." She paused, seeing the confusion in my eyes. Why would the fae go to the fortress? "They were dressed in their finest. I'm guessing they were going for—"

"The wedding." My gut turned into a pit of acid.

"I'm sorry," she whispered.

I shook my head. No, I wouldn't accept that. It couldn't be. Not yet.

I ran toward the fortress, with Ariella trying to keep up with me, but after a couple of minutes, my feet gave out and the breath was stolen from my lungs.

In the distance, the fortress loomed in the middle of the mountain, the shine of the setting sun casting ominous shadows on its dark stones.

And black and silver fireworks erupted in the sky.

Either the wedding had just started, or it had just ended.

I was too fucking late.

25

FARRAH

THE WHITE DRESS CLUNG TO MY BODY, ITS HEAVY SKIRT pulling me down along with the feelings churning inside of me. I halted in front of the closed doors to the main hall and took a deep breath.

Beyond these doors, the guests waited, and Prince Lark stood.

A chill ran down my spine.

Holy shit, I couldn't do this. I couldn't marry this tyrant. I couldn't shackle myself to him like this.

I inhaled deeply. But I had to. If I didn't, my people would be doomed, and I was tired of being selfish. My life didn't matter when it could save so many.

I took another long breath and nodded to the guards flanking the doors.

They pushed the doors open and announced my arrival.

The fae, dressed in fancy gowns and suits and cloaks,

flanked the long black carpet that had been rolled out from the doors to the dais. The dark path leading me to Prince Lark.

I ignored the whispers and the fake smiles as I walked down the aisle. My steps were firm, even though a turmoil grew inside of me. This would be a constant now, this mask I had to wear, and this lie I would live ... it would be forever now, and I had to start getting used to it.

I stared straight ahead, to a blank point on the wall at the end of the room, past Prince Lark, past the dais and his throne. It was the only way I would endure it.

But when I halted beside him just shy of the first dais' step, Lark reached for my hand and pulled me to his side, my shoulder pressed against his chest.

"My dear Farrah," Lark started, his voice barely above a whisper. His eyes followed a fae as he stepped into the dais and positioned himself before us. "Despite your willingness to be here, I think a warning is in order: behave and be a good wife, or I'll make your life a nightmare."

My breath caught. Didn't he know this was already a nightmare? I didn't like the threat, but it didn't change anything. "I was planning on behaving," I said, my voice equally low.

The fae in front of us smiled and opened his arm wide. "What a great day to celebrate this union!" He launched into a long speech about love and respect and foreverness, and I tuned him out, not willing to absorb any of his words. I might be here with my body, but my soul wasn't.

It would never be.

"Lady Farrah," the fae called out, snatching my attention. "Will you take Prince Lark of the Shadow Court as your husband?"

Lark's hand tightened slightly around mine.

As if I had a choice in the matter.

I sucked in a long breath and let it all out with two words that would probably become my doom.

"I do."

THANK YOU

Thank you for reading *The Wolf Forsaken*!

Reviews are very important for authors. If you liked my book, please consider leaving a review on your favorite retailers and/or on goodreads, please!

You can get the next two books on the series now:

The Fae Bound
The Blood Pact

Don't forget to sign up for my Newsletter to find out about new releases, cover reveals, giveaways, and more!

If you want to see exclusive teasers, help me decide on covers, read excerpts, talk about books, etc, join my reader group on Facebook: Juliana's Club!

THE FAE BOUND

Want a sneak peak from THE FAE BOUND? Continue reading ...

CHAPTER 1
FARRAH

THIS WAS SUPPOSED TO BE A PARTY, SO WHY I FELT ANYTHING but happy?

Seated at the throne that suddenly appeared beside Lark's at the main hall of the Shade Fortress after our wedding, I watched as the reception raged on. Even though it had been sudden, Lark had found a way to throw a huge party, complete with performers and fireworks.

The fae, all from the shadow court, indulged in the food and drink and dance, most already too drunk to even remember their name. Amid them all, Lark talked to other male fae. He laughed out loud and patted their backs, sometimes moving his arms wide, as if he too was drunk, but I knew better. He had been holding the same damn glass of champagne since the beginning of the party hours ago, and he had barely drunk a single sip so far. He was pretending to be drunk, though I had to admit he did look happy.

The complete opposite of me.

Every now and then, his dark eyes met mine from across the room, and it was all I could do not to flinch in disgust. But I kept it in. I held on his stare with a defiance of my own. Yes, I had married the fae prince, but that didn't mean I had to like it.

In fact, I despised it.

During the entire party, no one approached me. No one came to talk to me, except for a few servants who offered me food and drink. Still feeling sick about my unknown future, I refused those.

While the fae danced and chatted and drunk, I stayed seated and quiet on the throne, staring at the wall across the room, above everyone's heads, and counting the seconds.

Finally, when the sun was rising behind the mountain, Lark dropped his champagne flute and walked to me. By now, there only a handful of fae still dancing on the main hall, while most of them had already left, or slept on the floor, too drunk to care.

With an easy smile, Lark halted before me. "Ready to go?"

My stomach twisted in a million knots. No, I wanted to answer him. But I knew better than to tell him that. So when he offered me his arm, I stood from the throne chair and took it. Like a gentleman, he helped down the dais steps, then guided me over the black carpet cutting through the main hall. Outside, his guards waited. Once we walked by them, they counted five steps, then began following us.

I wasn't overly worried about the wedding night, because it was different for the fae. We had a rule called the Moon Period. The fae couldn't sleep together for three weeks after a wedding to seal the magical bond between them and wait for the mating bond to snap before trying to conceive a child, since creating a baby fae wasn't as easy as it was for humans.

Lark confirmed as much when he stopped in front of the closed doors to my chambers, his guards several steps back now.

The prince held both my hands this time. "I never thought much about the Moon Period until now." He stared into my eyes, the glint in his downright naughty. "But I understand its importance. I want to have many sons with you, Farrah, and I'll respect the Moon Period."

Two feelings warred inside me: relief that he wouldn't touch me tonight, but despair that soon the Moon Period would be over, and then I didn't know how I would keep him away from me.

What he didn't know, though, was that I couldn't give him any sons. Or daughters. Fae could only have children with those they had first been with, and for me that was Wyatt.

Wyatt was my mate and I hadn't even had the chance to tell him.

Even if I had the chance, would I have told him? There was no reason to make him more worried and sad about our situation. Not knowing he was my mate would help him move on faster.

Lark brought one of my hands to his lips and planted a kiss on my knuckles. "Sleep well, princess."

With a last lingering glance, he retreated. His guards followed, except for two, who positioned themselves on the hallways, a good way from my door.

Holding my chin high, I entered my chambers. But once I closed the door behind me, I broke down. Angry tears filled my eyes and I grabbed at the white dress, ripping it to pieces.

The tears slipped along with the pieces, scattering across the floor until I could barely see the smooth dark stone underneath. Only once I was free of that, I wiped my tears away and took a deep breath in.

No, I couldn't break down. Not now, not later. This was my life now and if I broke down now, what would happen to me for the rest of eternity? Because fae lived forever.

And Prince Lark was my husband forever now.

That knowledge, that fact, brought a sharp pain to my chest.

The idea of running away with the medallion fleeted through my mind, but I pushed away. Because running away wouldn't solve anything; it would only make things worse. But most of all, Lark wasn't an idiot. He had known I came to him using a medallion. He had taken it from me earlier.

But I had another thing he didn't know about it. I hurried to the closet, where earlier I had hidden the looking glass under some dresses, hoping no one would find it.

My hands shook as I held the looking glass.

I closed my eyes and willed it to work.

When I looked at it again, the glass had become a canvas swirling with smoke. I held my breath as the smoke cleared and the image took shape.

It was me, sitting in an armchair, wearing a long, blue dress, with a big smile on my face. I opened my arms and someone, a little boy, ran to me. He jumped on my arms and hugged me tight. When he glanced up at me, I could see it. The boy could be young, but he had Wyatt's hair, Wyatt's eyes, Wyatt's smile.

I almost dropped the looking glass.

What did this mean?

Then, the image was gone and the looking glass returned to its normal form.

"What the hell," I muttered shaking it, as if that would make it work. Usually, the damn thing showed three scenes, not just one.

I put the looking glass back into its hiding place and dragged my feet to the window. The sun was rising, tinting the mountain with orange and yellow light. For a moment, I closed my eyes and let the sun's warmth kiss my skin. If only life was this easy and kind.

But it wasn't. I leaned over the window and glanced down. The fortress stretched under my window, with many turrets and sharp points, and beyond it, was the harsh mountain.

From here, no one could resist a fall, not even a fae.

But killing myself wasn't the answer to this problem. Running away wasn't either.

Then how could I make my cursed life a little easier to bear? Become a dutiful wife and bow my head to Prince Lark? Not in a million years.

There was only one more solution I could see, one I had no idea how I would accomplish, but ... I couldn't just pretend I was a pretty doll. I couldn't just sit here and accept my fate.

Somehow, before the Moon Period was over, I was going to kill the prince.

CHAPTER 2
WYATT

THIS COULDN'T BE HAPPENING.

Even though I was sure Farrah was already wed to Prince Lark, I had tried entering the fortress many times, but every time I was stopped either by a horde of shadow fae soldiers guarding every entrance of the fortress, or by Ariella, who told me I would be killing myself.

She was right, I knew that, but I couldn't just give up. Beyond these trees, beyond the walls of the fortress, was Farrah. So close. There had to be a way of saving her from him.

"She doesn't need saving," Ariella said more than once. "She chose this."

I knew that too, but I couldn't believe that. I knew what Farrah was doing. She was sacrificing herself for her people. That hardly seemed fair.

After many botched attempts to sneak into the fortress, I let Ariella guide me deeper into the forest, where we wouldn't be found out by the shadow fae patrolling the area. She was sure they were expecting me and searching for me, with every intention to kill on sight.

I paced around the fallen tree trunk Ariella was seated at, my mind racing, my emotions buzzing, my blood boiling.

"Wyatt, you have been like that for hours now," Ariella said, her voice hard. For an angel, she was quite the tough one. "You have to stop and rest and relax if you want to keep going later."

I stopped, but I didn't relax. I glared at her. "I don't want to keep going later. I want to keep going now."

Ariella rolled her eyes, annoyed at me. Yes, I had been in this fucking state for hours now, and honestly, I couldn't see myself relaxing until I was able to rescue Farrah from the Shade Fortress.

"I know you want to *save* Farrah, and if you're so adamant about it, we will, but we can't just charge into the fortress now. It'll never work. We need another angle."

Fuck, she was right. I knew that. But it was hard to admit it.

With a heavy sigh, I finally succumbed and plopped down on the tree trunk beside her, the full force of my failure hitting me square in my chest. Holy fuck, I had let Farrah slip through my fingers and now she was the prince's prisoner.

There had to be something—

I slipped my hand inside my jacket and found something. Frowning, I pulled the blue stone Spencer had given to me before opening the portal for me. I stared at it.

"Do you have any idea what this is?" I asked, showing the stone to Ariella.

She took it from me, lifted up to the sky, turned it around. "Nope." She shook her head and returned it to me. "Why? It's supposed to do something? I couldn't sense any magic coming from it."

I raised an eyebrow at her. "Can you sense magic?"

"It depends. I never could pinpoint how it works, but sometimes I can feel magic coming from a person or an object." She shrugged. "There must be a rule, I just don't know it yet."

"Interesting," I muttered. I turned the stone around my fingers. "Anyway, an old fae gave me this stone before I came back. He told me to give this to Farrah. That it was crucial."

Ariella frowned. "How did he know about Farrah?"

"I have no fucking idea." I tucked the stone back into my pocket. "But if he knew about Farrah and me just like that, this means he knows more stuff, right?" I wanted to believe Spencer had some kind of super sixth sense, and he could predict something would happen. Like me taking the stone to Farrah would somehow help me in rescuing her. Otherwise, the alternative, that he was just plain crazy and came up with crazy things, was too disappointing.

"I'm afraid this Spencer guy is in the fae realm, though," Ariella said. "We can't get to him now."

Fuck, that was true. "What can we do then?"

After a moment of silence, Ariella glanced at me, the wheels inside her mind visibly turning behind her blue eyes. "What do you know about Blaze fae?"

"Just that they are one of the four more powerful kinds of fae in the fae realm, why?"

"Because I've heard about them before. When I was looking for the demons who took my wings, I heard there was a large camp of Blaze fae near the Grand Canyon, that they had come to hide after a big war they had against the shadow fae."

"So?" I asked, impatient about her point.

"So, if we can convince them to start the war again, but on Earth this time, we'll have help to rescue Farrah."

I shot to my feet. "They would do the heavy lifting for us."

Ariella stood before me. "Right."

A sense of purpose filled me. The Grand Canyon was far away from here, but if we got allies to help us fight, it would be worth it. Though it pained me to leave Farrah with Prince Lark, I knew he wouldn't hurt her. She would be safe for a couple more days.

"All right, then, let's go to the Grand Canyon."

I started marching toward the nearest road. Ariella caught up with me in no time, and we discussed a quick plan on the way. Steal a car, drive to the Grand Canyon, search for the blaze fae. If we didn't find them right away, we would try to find someone who had heard about them. Then we would convince them to fight the shadow fae stationed in the human realm.

But, before we reached the road, a group of women dressed in black clothes stepped in our way.

"Hello there," one of them said, with a toothy smile. "I'm Myra from the Bonecrown Coven."

My body stiffened. The Bonecrown witches. The ones that had kidnapped Farrah to use her in a blood sacrifice, but instead beat her up and let her to die alone in the forest.

Why the fuck were they here?

ABOUT THE AUTHOR

While USA Today Bestselling Author Juliana Haygert dreams of being Wonder Woman, Buffy, or a blood elf shadow priest, she settles for the less exciting—but equally gratifying—life as a wife, a mother, and an author. She resides in North Carolina and spends her days writing about kick-ass heroines and the heroes who drive them crazy.

Subscribe to her mailing list to receive emails of announcement, events, and other fun stuff related to her writing and her books: www.bit.ly/JuHNL

For more information:
www.julianahaygert.com

facebook.com/julianahaygert

twitter.com/juliana_haygert

instagram.com/juliana.haygert

goodreads.com/juliana_haygert

pinterest.com/julianahaygert

bookbub.com/authors/juliana-haygert

ALSO BY JULIANA HAYGERT

To find links and more info, go to:

www.julianahaygert.com/books/

Shorts

Into the Darkest Fire

Tested

Rite World: Blackthorn Hunters Academy

The Demon Kiss (Book 1)

The Hunter Secret (Book 2)

The Soul Bond (Book 3)

The Shadow Trials (Book 4)

The Infernal Curse (Book 5)

Rite World

The Vampire Heir (Book 1)

The Witch Queen (Book 2)

The Immortal Vow (Book 3)

The Warlock Lord (Book 4)

The Wolf Consort (Book 5)

The Crystal Rose (Book 6)

The Wolf Forsaken (Book 7)

The Fae Bound (Book 8)

The Blood Pact (Book 9)

The Wyth Courts

Winter King (Book 1)

Spring Warrior (Book 2)

Summer Prince (Book 3)

Autumn Rebel (Book 4)

The Fire Heart Chronicles

Heart Seeker (Book 1)

Flame Caster (Book 2)

Sorrow Bringer (Book 3)

Earth Shaker (Novella)

Soul Wanderer (Book 4)

Fate Summoner (Book 5)

War Maiden (Book 6)

The Everlast Series

Destiny Gift (Book 1)

Soul Oath (Book 2)

Cup of Life (Book 3)

Everlasting Circle (Book 4)